BLOOD & GUTS & HEXES

A CRYSTAL KINGDOM SHORT STORY COLLECTION

RAYMOND S FLEX

CONTENTS

B'LUBBID THE BONE FETCHER

"SIR?" the city guard said. "Do you mean, 'Belovèd?'"

B'lubbid the Bone Fetcher eyeballed the man, felt his throat get all caught in a knot, like whenever he had to speak with humans, and felt that same warmth rise in him.

That familiar warmth that would soon turn to a boiling mass of fury.

Why couldn't they get it right? Why did he have to explain *every* time?

Off over his shoulder he heard the *clop* of horses' hooves, and he knew, if he didn't get this matter cleared up in a timely manner that he would be asked, politely and crisply, to 'step aside,' to let the cart through.

Well, not today.

No, today, things would be different.

They'd remember him for all time.

And they'd remember his name.

B'lubbid reached for his cloak, felt the rough fabric of it, and he neatly flipped the hem of it to reveal his belt to the guard. And the dagger he kept there.

The dagger with the crooked blade.

He squinted at the guard, and let loose his shrivelly, uneven voice. The voice that he just *hated*. But, he was sure, after the cloven feet and the stubby horns sticking out through his stingy, greasy hair . . . or what passed for hair . . . the main feature that people who knew him recalled when picturing him in their minds.

If they could even remember his name, that was.

"Listen here, busy body, the name's B'lubbid *not* Belovèd, 'kay? No matter what your human books might say."

Much to B'lubbid's ire, the guard cracked a smile, and said, "You deal in rhymes, you lot, do you?"

B'lubbid screwed up his eyes. Of course he was speaking in the guard's language, *he* was the one making the effort here. And all he was getting thus far was wisecracks, and attitude. It was like they thought they could treat a bone fetcher just however they wanted.

He could almost smell that approaching stench of horse sweat, taste it at the back of his tongue. The *clickety-clack* of the cartwheels were like a hammer beating against his skull.

"Listen," B'lubbid said. "You gonna let me through, or what?"

The city guard continued to smile away, and, looking off down the road, apparently to the approaching cart, he waved B'lubbid through. As B'lubbid wiggled his way along, through the city gates, and into the jagged city of Flubbersmyre, the guard called out to him.

"And you take care with that dagger of yours, will ya? Might put someone's eye out with that thing."

B'lubbid muttered just about every curse known to a bone fetcher beneath his breath, and then focussed his attention to the relatively more important task of keeping his cloven hooves from becoming trapped between the cobblestones.

OVERHEAD, the sky was dimming, the sun was dipping down over the rooftops like a flaming tangerine, and B'lubbid felt that wonderful night-time chill pass over his hardened, leather-like skin.

He watched up ahead as a troupe of city urchins, all dressed in their raggedy clothes, danced in and out of the road, between the cart and horses, each time just about defying the large vehicles, managing to get out without a broken limb or worse . . . a broken neck.

A little further on, B'lubbid saw a pair of city guards, both with large sticks in their hands, oil-soaked rags aflame on the end of each, reaching up to light the night torches. Soon the streets would be flooded with that uneven, flickering firelight.

The kind of light that B'lubbid loved.

Because it was the great leveller.

B'lubbid could smell the burning oil carrying on the twilight breeze, and he breathed it in deep, filled his mouth with the tang of it, and he reminded himself of just how much he *loved* that scent.

It almost made all this interaction with humans worthwhile.

Almost.

As B'lubbid trudged on, already feeling a slight weariness catching up with him, after having, just like all the days, travelled down from the Sable Mountains, he felt the strain of his calf muscles, and several times his cloven hooves almost slipped between the cobblestones.

Thinking back, he wasn't all that sure whether the urchins saw him first, or if he saw them. He could be sure about one thing, however, and that was that *he* had been the first to look away.

To hurry on.

To try and slip into the shadows.

But it was too late.

"Oi, mister!" one of the urchins cried out.

B'lubbid kept his head down, feeling his pointed chin press into his bony chest. He wished to get on with his work, and to be gone from Flubbersmyre. He really had no business being around these humans for any longer than he had to be.

"Oi!" another of the urchins called.

B'lubbid quickened his pace, not wanting to show them that they'd got any sort of rise out of him. Oh, he was used to humans all right. In fact he could remember them from ever since he'd been a tiny, little bone fetcher.

They'd been the ones that'd chased him home, through the fields, back crying to his ma and pa. It always sent a flaming sense of a shame ripping through his stomach to think that he always sent his ma or pa out to see off the human children, to make them leave him in peace.

And here he was, an *adult*, for the gods' sake.

He heard the patter of their bare feet against the cobblestones, over his shoulder, and through his enormous flaring nostrils, he could smell that rancid odour of theirs.

That *human* odour.

All skin, and sweat, and muck, and nastiness.

The patter of their feet grew louder, and seemed to spring up on all sides of him.

There was one thing which he always cursed about him having been born a bone fetcher, and that was he was no match at all for a human in a race. Even a human child could easily outrun him over even ground.

A knife fight, though, that'd be a whole different matter.

Now he just needed to keep going. To ignore them. Just like his parents always told him.

He pressed onwards, stuffing his clawed hands in the pockets of his cloak, and trying to keep his face hidden from them, so that they might mistake him as just another human, perhaps a decrepit, foul, agèd human.

If they *believed* him to be a human then perhaps, just perhaps, they'd leave him alone.

And then he felt one of them tug at his cloak, grab it in their pudgy, grubby fist and give it a yank.

In that moment, B'lubbid lost all sense of his plan, of his attempt to evade the urchins, and he wheeled around, glaring, and peered at the urchins standing at his heels. "What do you *want*?" he said, pleased with the heat that came off his breath as he spoke.

The urchins all grinned at each other.

And, B'lubbid was pleased to note, they were all *nervous* grins.

"Where you off to, sir?" one of the urchins said.

B'lubbid took him in. By far the largest boy, he had blond hair, and fat, buttery cheeks, and about a thousand chins. He stood with his hands on his hips, and his grubby, sewage-stained cheeks seemed to give him shades of a fully-grown human.

Of a *man*.

Quickly, B'lubbid counted the rest of the urchins, and reached four in all, four which he could count on one claw. And he found himself caught up in brief, terrifying fantasies. Of jerking his hand upwards, and splaying his claws, catching each boy with his claw to their throat.

Watching the blood flow.

But that was no prospect. Not for him.

If the city authorities heard of any harm coming to a human by the hand of a mythical creature, then they would send out a party to the Sable Mountains, to burn down every village in sight.

And B'lubbid would not be responsible for so many deaths because he could not resist some light childish goading.

Which wasn't to say that it wasn't awfully tempting.

B'lubbid slowly turned back to the blond boy, to the leader, with that self-satisfied, smug expression of his, and he did his best to keep his voice level and in control, to give the impression of an adult being that should be treated with respect. "Why, I'm off to the city morgue, where else would you imagine a bone fetcher like myself to be headed?"

In that moment, one of the city guards lit up the torch just a few paces away, and it set the blond boy's face in profile in the fierce, auburn glow. B'lubbid noticed the dried bogies all sticking to the boy's upper lip, like sailors bailed out from their vessels following a tempestuous storm.

The blond boy sneered and then tilted his head back. He glanced round at his friends, no doubt for a touch of courage, just to have himself backed up in case the need arose.

B'lubbid knew of all the tales that the human teachers told their children. About the creatures of the night, the magical beings such as B'lubbid, and how they were all whipping tails, and organ-crunching teeth, and skin-ripping claws.

And yet all that indoctrination seemed to be having very little effect right now.

The boy stared back at B'lubbid, snorting up some phlegm, and then let loose a wad of spit. It fell onto the hem of B'lubbid's cloak.

B'lubbid glanced down to where the phlegm had landed, and for the longest time he felt himself rooted to the spot, rendered completely immobilised. And then, before he knew what was happening, he heard that cacophony of hucking spit, and the flurry of phlegm through the air.

He turned to run, or at least to stumble away from the boys, but he slipped and took a tumble. He landed on the cobblestones.

A spark of pain ran up his spine, and he let out a moan.

And just like that, the boys were upon him.

They were all kicks and punches, one of them bit him on the upper thigh.

If it hadn't been for his leathery, thick hide he might've been hurt, but as it was he forced himself to suck up all this abuse, letting the boys have their fun.

Humiliating though it was.

One of the city guards, lighting up the torch across from them, called out to the boys.

Immediately they all ceased.

B'lubbid glanced over to the guards, waiting for them to get the boys off him. The guards stepped closer to him, both still carrying that flaming wooden pole, its flames licking at the looming, mauve twilight sky. The flames flickered off their faces, bounced shadows between their cheekbones.

B'lubbid breathed in sharply, looked to the boys, their attention now drawn to the city guards, distracted.

"Come on, lads," one of the guards said. "Leave the poor beast alone, wontcha?"

The boys lingered about there, and B'lubbid caught the blond kid's face in profile, took in his narrow grin there, firmly pressed on his lips. He also saw that the blond kid clenched his fists down at his sides, ready to strike again at the moment that the city guards disappeared.

The city guard turned to B'lubbid and said, "Go on then, beast, you'd best hop it while you can."

B'lubbid wasted no time, swinging himself back up onto his cloven hooves and, just like that, swept his way off, down the road, and into the mounting shadows of the unlit streets.

He was safer in the darkness.

3

B'LUBBID CAME ACROSS the city morgue a while later. He took in the expansive, marble arches and the sturdy, gigantic wooden door, reinforced with iron, and he finally allowed himself to exhale.

He would be safe.

For the time being.

He walked up the steps, listening to the *clop* of his hooves against the stone slabs. He could already smell that stench of rotting flesh, clawing its way out from within the building. He licked his lips with his forked tongue, and felt his saliva moisten his mouth.

He knew that humans couldn't smell it, and if they could they would've picked a place far out of town to keep the morgue. Perhaps that would've been better for B'lubbid too, given that he wouldn't have had to venture into the city itself to fetch the bones.

He wouldn't have had that run-in with the children just now.

At the top of the steps to the morgue, he reached out and wrapped his gnarled fingers around the knocker, and he pounded it three times.

Just like always.

He listened to the scrape of the cane across the hearth inside the door, and soon enough he watched the door creak back in on itself, and the familiar figure of Hartly Tchunt standing there.

He was a man of about seventy or eight years, and he had a posture to match. His back seemed almost curved over on itself, and he constantly walked with his hand resting in the base of his spine.

B'lubbid wished him a good evening, and then stepped inside.

Hartly had wispy, silver hair which dangled right down past

10

his belly button, and his beard reached down to at least his nipples, or where B'lubbid imagined the man's nipples to be located.

Hartly carried a cane with a silver tip which scraped across all surfaces, and, when B'lubbid followed the man through the labyrinthine corridors of the morgue, he noticed the marks all over the stone floor, from the places where Hartly had walked over and over again: dozens of times a day, hundreds of times a week, and thousands and thousands of times a year.

B'lubbid didn't wish to think in decades, because, like most bone fetchers, he wasn't expected to live much past his twentieth year.

Hartly walked with a slight sway to his step, rocking back and forth as he made his way along the corridors, and his cane *tap-tapping* away the whole time.

B'lubbid supposed that Hartly was the closest person he had to a friend among the humans. But that wasn't unusual.

Humans and other creatures kept themselves apart.

And everyone seemed happy enough with that arrangement.

Humans stuck to their cities, their villages and towns, while other creatures preferred to stay among nature, so as not to forget themselves, so as not to forget just where they came from.

That they themselves *were* nature.

Hartly clambered his way down a stone, spiral staircase, taking the rail in his spare hand while his cane dangled from the other. He shuffled both feet onto each step before easing himself down onto the next.

B'lubbid often wondered what might happen to the city once Hartly died. Would they replace him with someone else? Hartly had no apprentice, nobody of that sort. Still, what did it really matter to B'lubbid, it was a human matter, not really for his consideration . . .

. . . And yet, he couldn't let the matter slip from his mind, for he knew that his own livelihood, that of his occupation and race, that of the *bone fetcher*, demanded that he be invested in whatever would happen to the mortuary.

When they reached the bottom of the staircase B'lubbid felt the symphony of odours carry him away. Those rotten stinks, the fruity flavour of the skin melting away, and, his favourite, the musky scent of the hair left unwashed.

He could hear a simple *drip-drip* coming from the main chamber of the mortuary, and he could hardly keep his mouth from watering.

He followed on Hartly's ankles, often having to remind himself that he had to be patient, that he had to linger back from him, take care not to step on the man's fragile heels.

Because the man was so frail B'lubbid's cloven hooves might break the man's bones.

And, just like that, before B'lubbid could wrap his head around it, they emerged in the main chamber itself.

And it was glorious.

B'lubbid gazed round him, to all the dead bodies, all the *dead* humans, all of them covered with white sheets. The sheets were stained green, brown, orange, black, and many more colours in between he would've liked to have got straight in his mind.

The petulance of the bodies was almost overwhelming now.

It made B'lubbid's gut churn, and his blood rumble through his veins.

He felt the sweat well in his pores, before overrunning and spilling down his skin, making his body slick, and moist.

That *drip-drip-drip-drip* sounded all round him.

He stood pinned to the spot, taking in all the bodies, all of them laid on their backs, beneath those sheets, lying flat on their wooden benches.

There must've been ten or eleven here this week.

And young, supple. A *contagious* disease, perhaps.

As if asking permission, B'lubbid turned and looked to Hartly, the old man, and he got a nod for his troubles.

As a courtesy, a lesson he'd learned long ago, he waited for the sound of the man's tapping cane, and frail footsteps to vanish from the main chamber before beginning his feast.

And, *oh*, was it a feast!

B'LUBBID SUCKED THEM all dry of their juices, munched his way through their chilled, bluish skin, and felt his gut almost burst out from within him as he gorged himself.

The odours wrapped themselves around his throat, pressed against the base of his tongue, and sent tingles dancing through every nerve in his body.

As he sucked up the final piece of gristle, disposed of the final knot of muscle, he laid the bones out in a large pile in the middle of the main chamber, and he looked to them, to those almost colourless bones before him, and he felt satisfied.

Deeply and truly satisfied.

And then he heard the familiar taping cane, and the steps of the old man, returning once more.

When he arrived in the doorway, the man refused to see the gore all spread out through the chamber, the blood lying in puddles all over the tiled floor, or even the pile of bones. He looked past them all. He looked to B'lubbid.

B'lubbid still tasted the rich flesh at the back of his throat, and he knew that he would be having dreams about this feast for weeks, nay, months to come. But in time it would fade. He had to savour every morsel he had eaten here so that when the northern wind blew against his mountain cottage, he could warm himself with these memories.

Still, despite the prospect of the frenzy, still ever-present in his mind, he managed to keep himself under control, to make his voice level and easy to understand.

Easy to understand for a *human*.

"I think this week I might need a cart for all the bones."

The old man's gaze seemed to slip off somewhere in mid-air,

before he snapped back to consciousness, and then the man turned and headed back off, away from the main chamber.

Away from B'lubbid, who stood there in the midst of it all, his heart pounding hard against his resilient ribcage and sucked it all up into himself.

THE OLD MAN brought the cart down through the double wooden doors into the basement of the morgue. B'lubbid watched him wheel the cart down through the catacombs, and listened to its wheels *eek-eek-eek* their way along the tiles. And even as he tried to meet the old man's eye, he met with resistance.

Why would no human look at him?

And if they did it was only with a wry smile.

He knew he was not inferior, that he should not be ashamed, and yet he could hardly take this another moment. These . . . these *vermin*. They were the ones who doomed B'lubbid and his kind, his fellow magical creatures, to the outskirts of the land.

And B'lubbid reminded himself to breathe, to tell himself that, in fact, they, the magical creatures, they were the true superiors of the world. For the humans had lost what they had once been. Now they were doing their best to escape nature.

To escape their *true* purpose.

B'lubbid reminded himself of what his ma and pa had once told him, that he and his kind, they were like the Moon, like the tides, like the endless pebbled beaches. Time would come and go, human civilisations would grow then crumble.

But they would always be there.

The magical creatures of the world would *always* remain.

Eek-eek-eek.

The old man, Hartly, brought the cart to a halt several paces away from B'lubbid. Perhaps he didn't want to get too close. Even after they'd worked together for all these years. B'lubbid supposed that Hartly had watched bone fetchers come and go, and had grown weary, if not accustomed.

Not even this man, the very pit of human organisation, the

carer of the dead, would show B'lubbid so much respect as to acknowledge him as a fellow creation.

But what did B'lubbid care?

He *was* the superior one.

B'lubbid set about his lonely task of piling the bones onto the cart. He took care, placing each one onto the cart, one by one, and he thought about what prices they would fetch him with the dark mages snuggled up there in the Sable Mountains.

All told it looked to be a great haul.

And B'lubbid knew that he should've been pleased.

Far more pleased than he felt.

When B'lubbid looked around he saw that the old man had slipped off somewhere. Now that he'd completed his work, seen to B'lubbid here, he supposed that he could drift off to sleep. Do whatever he wished now that he'd got shot of this most unpleasant of tasks. The consorting with *lesser* beings than he.

B'lubbid placed his hands on the harness of the cart and wheeled it back out through the catacombs, and into the half light of the city.

6

B'LUBBID WAS ABOUT half the way to the main gates of Flubbersmyre when he felt the prickle pass up his neck, cause his hairs to stand on end. And it was dramatic enough for him to think to put the cart down, and to look around him.

He breathed in the night-time air, took in the scents of the day. He breathed the vegetables, the manky smell of the onions, the sickly sweet lingering odour of apples, and a whiff of jelly wine too.

The things that humans consumed were enough to send shivers down his spine.

But the scents hadn't been enough to stop him.

No, there was something more.

B'lubbid removed his hands from the harness of the cart, inspected his calloused palms, where the splinters of wood had stuck into his skin. Those splints would be worth it. He would be rich with this haul of bones. So rich he might be able to stay away from Flubbersmyre for a while, not have to come back here.

No longer serve the humans.

That idea stuck with him. But could it be true?

He thought of all the feasts he might be missing out on, all the dead bodies he would miss out on consuming. And yet, couldn't he find somewhere else? If he couldn't stop himself serving humans then could he at least find another place. Somewhere smaller. A village, perhaps. A small town. Somewhere they still had a fearful awe for magical beings.

The more B'lubbid thought about, the more it made sense.

He *could* get away.

He had enough to get him on his feet, to allow him to travel, to know the world.

To find something better.

And it was with that thought emblazoned on his mind, that he heard the distinct *whistle* of an object through the air. An object which struck him right in the temple. And which, when it skittered down onto the cobblestones at his feet, he established to be a rock.

A *sizeable* rock.

7

B'LUBBID SPUN ROUND on the spot, looked all about him, trying to establish from which direction the attack had actually come. But all he could see was the darkness, augmented slightly by the occasional torch hanging from the stone walls, shedding uneven orange light over the emptied city streets.

He stayed still, where he stood. He felt the warm ooze of blood trickle down from his temple, settle on his skin, and, finally, make his cheek slick. But he didn't raise his hand to wipe it off. He wanted to scope out his attacker.

To know just who he was.

And then, out the corner of his eye, B'lubbid caught sight of movement. Off in a nearby side-alley, on the other side of the street.

Without thinking twice, he shot off from his spot, and danced his way across the cobblestones, listening to his cloven hooves patter back at him in the form of echoes.

8

B'LUBBID TORE ROUND the corner and into the alley, already reaching for the dagger with the crooked blade at his waist. And he unsheathed it, held it down at his side, ready to snick whoever needed to be snuck, to teach whoever needed teaching a lesson.

He slunk through the darkened alley, hearing his heart bound and leap in his chest, making his hand shake a little where he held the dagger down at his side.

Another rock struck him.

Stars dotted his vision, and he felt the pain pulse through his cranium, but he stifled any groan that threatened to emanate in his throat, and he stalked on. Now sure to have a lock on his tormentor. And then—*yes!*—he could see the man, right there, lingering in the corner of the alley, thinking he was hidden in the shadow.

B'lubbid kept his pace slow, not wanting to attract the man's attention. He remained sleek and swift in his movements, and when he came to walk past where the man hid, B'lubbid moved so quickly, so decisively with his blade, that he slit the throat before the man even had the chance to stand up straight to him.

As the humans said: *to face him like a man.*

Such a ridiculous expression.

And B'lubbid felt the blood welling, this time the man, felt it come first as a rivulet and then as a torrent, dripping down at their feet. Forming a puddle.

B'lubbid retreated from the man, stood back.

Up above the alley, the Moon emerged from behind a thick cloud and shod its half light over them down there. And B'lubbid saw the man's face.

Not a man at all.

The child.

The boy from earlier.

Just the blond boy.

And yet, B'lubbid felt no pity as he watched the boy, eyeballs rolled back in their sockets, as he slid down the wall, and then fell into a crumpled heap there. The blood still spurting out from him.

So he had killed his tormentor.

That would be another one for Hartly to worry about.

Another body.

And the bones, well, B'lubbid couldn't help himself. He knew that he was never coming back.

Never to Flubbersmyre.

And so he sucked all the boy's goodness out and then spat him out, just as he'd spat on B'lubbid. And then he took the boy's bones off to his cart, and piled them up on the rest. He listened to them clank and jostle into place. Forever lost among all the other bones there.

B'lubbid drew his cart out through the sleeping city, listening to the *clank* and *crank* of the wheels as they found, and then bounced out of, the cobblestones. And before he knew it he was out through the main gates, back out onto the plains.

And headed for the Sable Mountains.

And into a fresh, new life.

ONDERSWORT

T HE HORSE-DRAWN prison wagon careened along the crude dirt road, threatening to be tossed off into one of the expansive ditches, at either side, at any moment.

A ragged man of seventy or more, the driver, had winding silver hair which coiled back over his shoulders in the rush of air pouring over the wagon. He arched his back and brought the reins down on the backs of the half dozen, beaten up horses, flanks gleaning with sweat, mouths sprouting white foam, their collective breath hoarse as pumping bellows.

The sable night outside made no effect on Edmund Dunnay, who sat inside the tarpaulin tent of the prison wagon, crouched in the corner, knees clenched to his chest. The air stank of excrement and sweat, and a clamminess clung to everything—sweat seemed to seep out of the very wooden planks of the wagon.

Edmund closed his eyes, straightened and pressed his back up against the iron bars, the pain they effected on his spine long having descended into a mundane numbness, and he did his best not to touch any of the other slumped human forms sharing this mediocre space. There must've been at least twenty, maybe thirty, all crammed into this one spot.

"What you in fer, stranger?"

A twitch skittered up Edmund's spine. Throughout the journey thus far, several weeks, he had kept himself away from his fellow prisoners . . . no that wasn't what they were, that had been put very clearly to them when they had left Ilsnare, the Crystal City, behind—no they were immigrants now, of a kind . . . in any case, whether the others be *immigrants* or crooks, he had little interest in fanning the flames of any fledgling friendship.

"Got cloth for ears or what, pal?" the stranger uttered.

Edmund kept his eyes shut for as long as he thought he could —as long as he could get away with, without the stranger jibing him once more. Just as he could sense the stranger drawing breath, he swallowed back his dry spit and opened his eyes into narrows slits and peered out.

As much as Edmund could establish in the gloom of the prison wagon, he made out a round form of the stranger—or perhaps he wore a bulky coat, mad in this baking space—and a twinkle from one of his eyes, reflected from where the Moon penetrated through a slight gap in the tarpaulin of the gaoler's cart.

"Does it matter?" Edmund said.

Edmund thought he made out the approximation of a shrug from the stranger, and then the stranger said, "You gotta done something ta get sent ta Onderswort."

Edmund neglected to answer.

"Come now, most likely we'll find ourselves neighbours when we get there, in the very least fellow citizens, so what could just a little story-telling do wrong?"

Edmund ran his fingers along the calluses which cratered the insides of his fingers, what had once been baby-soft skin.

The wagon jerked to the side. The sound of rocks and loose dirt splattered up against the outside of the tarpaulin. The bodies in the wagon wobbled about. Edmund almost lost his balance, but found himself before he tumbled. A heartbeat later and he realised that it was the stranger who had kept him steady, his arm reaching out and holding him up, pressing back against Edmund's chest.

The stranger held steady another few seconds and then, with a grin, released him. "See?" the stranger said, refinding his own spot. "That's what good having a friend can do ya. Now whatta you say? Why're you here on this wagon?"

Edmund steadied himself, this time twining his hardened

fingers around the iron bar behind him. He was determined that whenever the wagon took another bounce there would be no need for a reassuring hold. He could manage on his own. Of that he was sure.

Realising that he would have to give the stranger some kind of answer, some motive, he said, "Stealing."

Someone in the wagon coughed, another spat. Whether they'd overheard Edmund's remark, which he'd spoken at almost a whisper, wasn't certain.

The stranger gave him a nod. "A'ight," he said. "If that's what you wish me to believe."

Feeling a little put off by this slight, Edmund added, "That's the truth."

"Nah," the stranger said, shaking his head. "That's not enough. They wouldn't go to the trouble of sending you to Onderswort if cleaving off one of your hands would be just as suitable punishment."

"You call *this* trouble?" Edmund said, indicating the wagon.

The stranger laughed dryly. When he composed himself, he said, "Why yes, yes I do."

"And what makes you think they wouldn't send a thief to Onderswort?"

Outside, one of the horses whinnied and Edmund sensed the wagon picking up speed—they were going downhill. Hooves slipped and clobbered at the dirt road, stuck between an urgency to move forward as quickly as possible and an urge for some stability under foot.

The stranger leaned closer, his halitosis growing more sour in Edmund's nostrils, taking precedence over the rest of the musky odours of the wagon. "Onderswort is at the very edge of the empire—*the* border town. Beyond Onderswort there ain't nothing but wild. Bogs, swamps, fields of reeds. You'll find nothing. Wasteland that'd make Onderswort look like a cultural hotbed.

"Onderswort itself, why it's nothing but a few crooked, miserable old shacks, slumped one against the other—very much like how we are right here in this wagon.

"In the winter there's snow up to yer neck, in spring a grey mist smothers the place, in summer, well it gets hot, but that's when the horlicks get to hunting, what with those sleek, leathery bodies and great big, razor-sharp teeth, and that taste for human flesh. Then the autumn blows it all away and you start again.

"Now, tell me, friend, what would a thief get out of that?"

"Get out of what?"

The stranger loosed another dry chuckle. "Why, the boredom, the desperation, the constant fear of death?"

"Isn't a thief just like any other criminal?"

"Of course he is. Just not the sort that gets sent to Onderswort."

"Then what type of criminal does get sent to Onderswort?"

The stranger steeped himself in silence as if in consideration of exactly how he would phrase his next words, and then he said, "A *political* one."

I N THE MORNING, after yet another sleepless night, the wagon drew to a stop, its wheels creaking as the driver applied the brakes. The tarpaulin flipped open and the driver took stock of those inside. Bright sunlight streamed into the prison wagon and the cold, fresh air was like a tonic, washing away all the horrendous odours.

Edmund took several gulps of air and then stared back into the driver's eyes, his pale green eyes, the only aspect of his appearance which suggested he had once been young. The driver took a rasping breath and then shoved a jug of spilling water between the bars, into Edmund's chest.

Edmund took it from him, only realising the extent of his thirst when he touched the neck of the bottle to his lips. He finished about an eighth of the jug and then handed it over to the stranger, who was just blinking himself round from, somehow, managing to sleep.

The stranger accepted the jug with a smile. He wiped his lips when he'd drunk his fill and passed it onto the next prisoner in the wagon. "You not come round to telling me all about what you done, then?"

Edmund looked out through the bars. He supposed they were drawing closer to Onderswort. The landscape itself was fairly flat, lots of swampland and towering tufts of grass. As the stranger had commented earlier about the spring, there was a grey mist hanging over the landscape around them, and now that he'd got over the initial ecstasy of the fresh air, he admitted to himself that it was certainly kicking up a chill. A real bite to it. He shivered, crossed his arms over his chest and rocked back and forth.

The stranger snorted back his snot. "At least level with me. You ain't no thief, are you?"

Edmund picked out a single, withered and leafless tree on the horizon, its twisted and shrivelled branches reminding him of deformed human limbs. It seemed as though the very environment, this *place*, had beaten that tree down, left it like that.

What might it do to him?

The stranger elbowed him in the ribs. "Eh?"

Edmund turned his attention back to him. "No, I'm not a thief."

"There we go. Least we're gettin' somewhere now."

A silverbird swooped through the air, dive bombing the prison wagon, before shooting back upward, into the greying sky. It emitted a light twitter as Edmund lost its form among the rest of the dreariness.

The driver removed the jug of water and tied it back up to the wagon. He hauled himself up onto the wagon and back behind the horses, whose breath wafted before them in hazy clouds.

Edmund wished he could slip between the bars and run, right out into those long grasses, be done with it. But he would have no freedom. Not until they arrived in Onderswort.

The wagon bounced onward, along the narrowing and poorly maintained dirt road.

The stranger lurked beside him, staring out at the hedgerows passing them by. He looked wistful, and he appeared much younger than Edmund had presumed from their conversation the previous night. He had a few wrinkles and, like his own, the areas around his eyes were sunken pits, but, he supposed, the stranger was about the same age as he was.

Perhaps they had more in common than he had suspected previously.

The wagon lurched onward, making its way along the

increasingly winding road. Edmund gazed out onto the horizon, trying his hardest to get the first glimpse of Onderswort: the end of the line. And then, all of a sudden, a rogue tear snaked its way down his cheek and splashed on his trouser leg. He turned his face away from the stranger, but it was too late—he had already seen.

"Leave your family behind?" the stranger asked.

Edmund nodded.

"Yup, me too, hardest thing I ever did."

When Edmund turned back to face the stranger, he saw that he'd taken up a wistful expression, no doubt the faces of those family members—a wife, children?—forever etched on his mind's eye. And Edmund's heart warmed for him, because he had suffered the same.

What really tore Edmund apart was that, with every hour they'd passed on the boat, those weeks it had taken them, with each tossing of the waves, he had noticed the feeling growing fainter and fainter: distance was like cotton wool, cushioning him against the effects of nostalgia, and now here he was well on the way to Onderswort.

When he arrived would his affection for his family be forever lost?

The stranger squeezed Edmund's shoulder. "We'll be there for each other, eh? This is our domain now." He leaned back, looked over the rest of the prison wagon, the dreary faces all wrapped up in rags. "Never say never, who's to say we won't be back there one day—Ilsnare."

Edmund sunk his teeth into his lower lip and fought back yet more tears. Slowly, he met the stranger's eye. "I wasn't into anything, you know, bad. Never was all that interested in politics, to tell the truth. They just . . . I don't know, I kind of fell into it."

The stranger gave him a rugged smile. "I think, in a way, we all fell into it. There's no shame. Not here, down in the pit of the world, in Onderswort. We're all of a kind."

"Yeah, I suppose you're right."

They slipped into silence, the easy silence of a decade-long friendship. And the wagon wheels crunched onward, creaking their way uphill and squeaking down again. The reins cracked against the backs of the horses and the driver's leather boots squeaked against one another.

Edmund passed into a trance, watching night fall on their surroundings. He had descended into an uneasy half-sleep when he sensed the wagon coming to a halt—the horses' hooves coming to rest and the driver muttering curses to himself as he eased himself off his seat. He listened to the driver's footsteps as he rounded the wagon and then tore off the tarpaulin to lay the passengers bare to the glare of burning torches all around.

Edmund brought his arm up to his eyes to guard against the brightness.

The driver seized the key which hung by a hefty chain around his neck and stabbed it into the hardy padlock which kept them trapped within the prison wagon. The ancient mechanism groaned and then gave way. He tossed the padlock to the ground where it landed with a dull *thump*. He yanked the wagon door downward and its hinges protested with a rusty *squeak*. He stood to one side, stared in at them and said, "Welcome to Onderswort, ya miserable bastards, though bastards ya may be you're prisoners no longer. This is your home now."

A sudden, unexpected nausea gripped Edmund. He found himself on his haunches, dry retching in the corner of the wagon. He felt the sure touch of the stranger on his back.

"Come on," the stranger said. "You'll be better for some rest and some hot soup inside ya."

Edmund rested on his knees for several seconds then cast his glance upward to the stranger. He managed a deranged smile and, shaking all over, got to his feet with the stranger's aid.

Together they trudged off the wagon and set foot down on the dirt—the dirt which looked just as it had for the entire journey in the gaoler's cart, but this was different because now they were free men once again.

The hard ground acted like an elixir on Edmund, and he felt refreshed, ready to stand on his own. He cast off the stranger's hold and gazed at the village which surrounded him. Grim though it was, no more than shacks cobbled together from cast-off wood and a few knackered nails, there was *some* hope.

And then, overhead, hanging like a phantom over the road which had brought them to Onderswort, he saw the Moon. He recalled that it was one and the same as the one which hung over Ilsnare. And he declared to himself, then and there, that he would be back one day.

But it would take time.

Here in Onderswort, time was the one thing he did have.

The stranger's voice took on a gruff, more serious tone. "Over there, do you see? There's a good old inn, they'll serve us a hearty soup. You'll be all the better for it, I swear. This ain't the time for remembrance, brother, we gotta look to the future, yeah?"

Edmund permitted himself another few precious seconds of gazing at the moonlight and then, feeling his saliva dampen his mouth, he turned and smiled at the stranger.

They walked together toward the inn, taking no care to avoid the puddles which dotted, what must've been, the town square— their tattered excuses for boots long ago having become sodden with a mixture of rainwater, blood and puss.

Edmund cast off his urge to glance back for the last time over the shoulder, instead stepping onward, over the threshold into the warm interior of the inn where a fire burned and crackled merrily.

3

OUTSIDE, the driver learnt up against the prison wagon, running his fingers along the base of his chin feeling the engrained moles and abscesses, winding his fingertips in and out of his wiry beard when he grew appalled at their touch.

How had he grown so old, so fast?

He looked on at the inn for a while and then mounted the wagon. He paused with the reins raised in his hands and then brought them down on the backs of the horses, bringing them back round to the beginning of the long road back to the port, where the boat from Ilsnare would leave him a not-so-fresh batch of citizens: more criminals.

He would not stay the night in Onderswort.

Tonight, like every other night heading back to the port, he would pitch a camp halfway, sleep beneath the stars and the Moon, away from everyone. He was a mere vessel—a means to an end—but he had never betrayed the kingdom, and he never would. He was a proud servant and was honoured to do his duty.

As he proceeded along the road, feeling those old familiar bumps and creaks of the wagon below him, part of him as much as the aches in his back or the sores on his arse, he grinned to himself. The people of Ilsnare could rest easy tonight. He would keep these people to the fringes, just as they needed to be.

He would keep the true citizens safe.

THE HOBBLESMAN

I

M AVE'C TROD THROUGH the mounting snow dunes. He gazed upwards at the mountains towering above him, as if threatening to tumble down at any moment. He felt the chill of the stiff breeze blow through his ragged working hand's clothes, and his heart throb at the base of his throat.

The air was fresh, at least that much could be said of it, but at the same time it seemed stripped of anything familiar. If it had ever carried the scents of honey suckles or of summer long grass, those were long gone now. Replaced by an all-out, mind-numbing frosty edge.

He listened to the snow crunch beneath his boots, and the breeze shriek through the mountain passes above him. He was sure to find something soon. He just had to keep walking.

Keep going on his way.

His mind was still thick of summer thoughts, of bringing in the yield with the sun on his back, warming his shoulder blades, and that ever-present glimmer of sweat on his face, those sweaty droplets snaking their way, one by one, down the collar of his tunic.

But thoughts could only give so much, provide so much respite before the cold came back in. He could feel it right down to his bones, icing them over, turning them brittle and useless. And yet he still found the strength to put one foot in front of the other.

He drew his scarf tighter round his mouth and neck, feeling his breath warming the wool, making it moist. He watched each of his breaths cloud out through the narrow-weave of the scarf and hang there before him—sometimes, in his more mind-addled moments, he thought of it as his soul leaking right out of him. Not that he believed in that mystic claptrap.

Not really.

He trod onwards, his muscles aching, drawing tight then contracting, his mind becoming more and more disillusioned with the mountain white cropping up on all sides. But he only had eyes for the road before him. The pristine snow that opened up ahead. He knew, several feet below, there was a cobbled path. Every so often he felt its jagged stones against the tread of his boot. It felt like some god drawing him on, reassuring his every step. He thought of the legends of the mountain ghosts, and wondered if there was any truth to it.

Back there in the fields he never would've given it a moment's thought.

But he wasn't in the fields now, was he?

The path wound its way round the mountain. And he knew, or he'd been told, that on the other side of the mountain there was opportunity. Another job for an elderly working hand like him. A job for the springtime, and the summer coming. If he was lucky they might take him on till the autumn. When this winter blew itself out, he would be fifty, and on his knees.

He had no family, no home. Not uncommon for an orphaned man like him. He needed to travel to where the work was. This was his life.

His feet weighed heavy as he rounded the mountain path. As he kept himself level, and tried to keep his mind bright and alert. If he forgot himself, gave into the cold, that would be the end. He would freeze to death right out here on this mountainous path.

As the snow fell in thick flakes all round him, he saw a dim glow just around the corner.

Torchlight. Firelight.

It made the snow glisten yellow. He could almost feel its warmth right now. Feel it tickle his cheeks and wrap round his chest.

He swallowed against his dried-up mouth, trying his best to get some moisture back in there. He needed water. And food. Shelter. He was all out here alone, and he would die without sustenance. The snow had come so suddenly, and so quickly. He knew it was his fault. He had waited far too long back at the last farmer's fields, waited too long for a job that he knew deep down was never coming.

And now it might cost him his life.

He quickened his pace. His feet dipped in and out of the snow dunes, barely touching the cobblestones below the soles of his boots. The snow was thicker here. He yanked his legs back out, shook them free of the clinging snow, and stepped onwards.

And then, feeling the snow snatch hold of his ankle, drag it behind him, down into the freezing, crisp, feather-light flakes, he felt himself falling. He fell sideways. Down into the snow dune.

And before long the whiteness, the profound chill, was all-consuming.

2

A CRACKLE. A hum. Warmth.

Mave'c opened his eyes.

He stared out through the narrow slits, his eyelashes making his surroundings blurry.

He blinked once.

Twice.

The world around him came clearer, but remained distant. And the warmth grew more distinct. Less a tickle at his chest and more a thick and insulating blanket. He hunched his shoulders, and drew his arms up. He felt the fabric of the material. Lamb's wool. Nothing like the frayed material of his scarf. This was beautifully smooth, and felt like warmed butter against his skin.

He breathed in, caught a lungful of soothing woody smoke. He thought of his pipe and, still in a daze, padded his person, the chest pocket of his tunic. But he found nothing. He wasn't wearing his tunic. Just the blanket, and clothes that didn't belong to him.

He looked about him. Took in his surroundings.

A furnace stood a few paces away from him, its flames flickering through the window in its steel casing which was charred and dented from use. Another wave of heat wafted over him. He felt it warming his blood.

Bringing him back to life.

He thought back to his last memory. Out there in the snow. Climbing up the mountain. And then it'd all gone black. Now he was here.

The walls were made of wood. He could almost feel the softness of the wood. Of the light brown colour soothing him. And then, reaching out below him, he felt the soft wood of the bench there. A straw mattress beneath him. At his head his fingers stumbled over a well-stuffed pillow. His fingertips wormed their way inside and brushed against the feathers there.

Goose feathers.

He tilted his head, looked to the door. Shut tight. To his other side he saw a curtained window, and felt a brief chill tickle his neck as he thought of what it must be like outside.

But where was he now? And who had brought him here?

Just as he pondered those questions, he heard gentle footsteps sound outside his door, that unmistakable slap of sandal against stone. And, even before he watched the door creak open on its hefty, steel hinge, saw the figure dressed in those familiar light brown robes. With that shaved head. And then he knew just where he was.

A monastery.

M AVE'C'S BREATHING SLOWED, and his heart did too, as he stared at the monk darkening the doorway to his bedroom. He felt that same chill that had passed through him outside on the mountain path as he looked over the man standing there.

The monk wore a neutral expression. His cheeks were plump and slightly rosy. And his eyes twinkled a little reflecting the light from the flaming furnace. He might've been portly or thin as a spear, but the way that his robes hung off him, draping off him, made it impossible to either confirm or deny his true stature.

Mave'c drew another breath, tried to calm himself. His eyes rested on the monk, and he waited for him to speak. The monk finally did.

"We found you, out there on the mountain," the monk said.

Mave'c could only manage a nod and a slight groan. As he tried to shift himself into a sitting position he realised that he was much weaker than he had imagined.

"You must be starving," the monk said.

This time Mave'c managed a frail, and raspy, "Yes."

The monk nodded. Although Mave'c couldn't be entirely sure, he thought that he saw a faint smile cross the man's lips. But before he could get a second glance, the monk slipped out from the doorway, and disappeared.

Mave'c was left only to stare out into the deserted corridor.

Out into the darkness of the monastery.

4

THE MONK RETURNED with another monk, a much younger monk.

If Mave'c had to guess, he would've pinned the younger monk at around thirteen, maybe fourteen years old. Although he was bald, like the others, Mave'c could see the boy's natural hair colour was blond, his eyebrows were that faint mousy colour.

The younger monk carried the woven wicker tray in his hands with a bowl of soup steaming away on top. A small basket of warm bread wrapped up in a piece of cloth, and smelling strongly of honey. Beside it there was a chunky porcelain mug steaming away too.

Mave'c caught a whiff of those smells, felt them thicken in the air. Potatoes, hearty splashings of the mountain herbs the monks clearly grew up here. And then, he sniffed again just to be sure . . . yes, it was wild berry tea. That delicious tea the monks grew, and that he'd tried once several years before, something a lady in a passing village had offered him on the way to another job.

The younger monk set the tray down beside his mattress, on the wooden bench, and then he retreated to stand in the doorway, beside the first monk.

Mave'c gave them each a weak smile of gratitude, and then, feeling a little uncomfortable having the two of them watching over him, but not so much that it would affect his hunger, he dug into the soup.

5

A S MAVE'C MOPPED UP the remnants of his soup with the warm, honey-flavoured bread, he looked between the two monks. His eyeballs felt stiff in their sockets, strung out with fatigue. "Thank you," he said, feeling his throat warmed from the soup. "Thank you so much."

Again, the first monk gave him that faint hint of a smile.

Mave'c popped the last piece of bread into his mouth, and then slurped the last of the tea.

The wild berries were beyond all imagination. Just truly past all that his memory could provide him. Up here, in the mountains, in this mountain monastery, he supposed it was more potent, that the berries were fresher. He almost lost his mind to the sickly sweetness of the berries. And it was wonderful.

The monk stepped out from his place, approached Mave'c and relieved him of the tray, which, in turn, he handed off to the younger monk standing there.

The younger monk gave the older monk a half bow and then left the room.

Mave'c listened to the slap of the monk's sandals against the stone slabs of the corridor outside, until they drifted into nothingness.

He turned his attention back to the monk, still watching over him, that twinkle in his eye from the reflected flames of the furnace. He felt a lump form in his throat. Of course he'd heard all about monks, knew just what they were about. And he wouldn't be being sincere to himself if he didn't admit that, by coming up here, into the mountains, by making his way to the promised job on the other side of the mountain range, he hadn't privately nursed the thought. What else did he have to live for? Would he be damned to wander the plains searching for yet more opportunities as a working hand till the day he dropped dead?

. . . Or might he become a monk?

Mave'c looked to the monk standing over him. "I . . . I suppose that I really had nowhere else to go. If you hadn't found me—*saved* me, then I might've died out there, in the snow."

The monk simply inclined his head, again that shred of a smile crossed his lips.

Mave'c felt his strength coming back to him. The glow of warmth from the furnace made him salivate, and that thick woody smell remained in the air. He listened to the *crackle* and *crunch* as the logs shifted inside the furnace.

"Some of us are wanderers," the monk said. "Some us of us never settle down any place. We keep on moving."

Mave'c allowed himself a half smile. "You mean, you were like me? You wandered around the world too?"

The monk inclined his head, suggesting a nod, but neither confirming or denying it completely.

"What . . . were you like me? A working hand? Going between the fields?"

"Many of us have worked the fields."

Another shred of hope flowed through Mave'c. He felt his heart rise into his throat, and his gut churn with the nourishing soup and bread congealing there.

A log crunched inside the furnace and flames spat up through the gap in the steel casing.

Mave'c looked back to the monk. "And do you think that I could become one of you—that I could become a monk?"

The monk gave Mave'c a slight smile.

6

OVER THE NEXT FEW DAYS Mave'c grew accustomed to life at the monastery. He learned its name from one of the monks: Ravensbark. He liked the sound of it. And he watched on as the clear blue skies opened up over the monastery. The sun shone down on everything, made the snow glisten. But the ice refused to melt. And the packed snow made the mountain pass impassable.

One of the monks informed Mave'c that he might be permitted to stay at Ravensbark till the snow melted, till the mountain path opened up again, and he could continue his journey, move on his way to his next job as a working hand. And yet, Mave'c was determined to prove himself, to show them that he could be one of them.

There was magic and mystery about the place, and he wished to be a part of it. He wanted to serve his retirement here. He wanted to live out the rest of his life as a monk.

Whenever he asked the question he received an evasive response. Sometimes he would stand out in the corridor outside his room, his elbows resting against the ornate railing and stare down into the courtyard down below. He would watch the monks go about their business, to their morning prayers, and to their afternoon chores.

In the evenings he'd watch them light their candles out on the periphery of the monastery, to guard against mountain ghosts and other threats to the peace and tranquillity of Ravensbark.

He loved those rituals, those steady routines, and they became part of him as much as he breathed. And more than once he would stop monks on their way, along the corridor, brushing past him, and ask them what he must do to be like them.

Most would give him a faraway smile, with that same glint in their eye, and tell him to take up the matter with the Abbot, with the monk who had welcomed him to the monastery.

To the monk that he had learned was called Damon Shriversmyth.

7

IT WAS ANOTHER early evening, between the chores and the candle-lighting, when Mave'c decided that now was his time to make his wishes known. He had become more and more familiar with Ravensbark during his stay. Whereas before its twisting alleys of stone, and its creeping vines, iced over, had before been an unsolvable enigma, now they presented him with clues on getting about. And he floated from point to point, finding his way from one jutting stone to the next, until he found the unmistakable location of Damon's office.

The Abbot's office door was distinct from the rest of the doors along the corridor because of the sculpted raven sticking out from it, spreading its wings, its beak jutted open and the hint of its tongue showing from inside.

Mave'c had often regarded the raven on his exploration of the monastery, and he'd found it almost impossible to look the sculpted creature in its smoothly carved eyes for too long.

Something about birds, about the way they fluttered, their calls, had always put him on edge. He never trusted them. Perhaps, somewhere in the recesses of his mind, there was some childhood memory which they triggered.

Or maybe his fear was as unfounded as a delirious nightmare.

He reached up for the large, brass knocker and brought it hammering down twice.

Over his shoulder, Mave'c heard the knock reverberate around the courtyard, an icicle tinkle onto the stone ground. His hair stood on end and he felt the gentle sting of the crisp winter's wind against the nape of his neck.

The door drew back, Damon stood there and, with that same faint smile, invited Mave'c in.

8

MAVE'C SAT in the cushioned, high-backed chair which sat facing Damon, who sat behind his desk, that same slight smile on his lips, with his hands clasped before him, clearly waiting to see what it was that Mave'c had to say.

Mave'c saw no reason to delay, so he came out with his wish, as plainly and simply as he could. And then he sat there, listening to the silence tumble all around them, waiting for Damon's response.

The monk's smile never waivered from his lips as he considered the request, and his reply was just as composed, as long-thought over, as that smile. "We monks, we sit between two realms of magic, you do understand?"

Mave'c nodded in reply to Damon's question.

"Fire and ice, the two grand realms of magic in the world, and where we, the monks, sit is a greatly vulnerable place." He widened his eyes, and raised his finely-haired eyebrows. "Perhaps looking around here, looking around Ravensbark, you might be mistaken in thinking that ours is a life of peace and wellbeing. That this is a quiet place where we shelter from the pressures and strains of the real world." He shook his head. "But nothing could be further from the truth, believe me."

Mave'c smelled wild berries in the air in the room, made all the thicker by the open fireplace over in the corner of the room, and he felt the sensation tickle his throat, loosen his inhibitions.

He knew all this. He had heard all the stories of magic on his travels from job to job. And although he heard what Damon said, about them sitting between the two precariously balanced forms of magic, it never occurred to him for a second that this was anything other than hyperbole.

After all Mave'c thought to himself that people were always

given to exaggerate their role in the world. And he supposed the monks, for all their humility, their simple way of living, a shred of pride flowed strong through them all.

They wouldn't let just anyone in.

Now, more than ever, he knew just what he wanted, and he had to open and honest. He knew for himself that now, having seen how the monks lived, having stayed up here in Ravensbark, that he could never willingly allow himself to leave.

Or be made to leave.

Damon shifted his hands off his desk, and laid them down on his belly. Then he broke off eye contact with Mave'c, and stared at his stubby fingers. "It's all very well to wish for something, but it's an entirely different matter for it to come true." He glanced up at Mave'c, that same twinkle in his eye from the firelight. "Are we agreed?"

"Yes," Mave'c said, feeling his throat rough from the warmth, and the promise of comfort and a life beyond that of the back-breaking hard work of the working hand that Ravensbark offered him.

Damon's smile faltered, and then he looked back to Mave'c.

Mave'c felt an icy chill enter the room, and he was sure that it was a draught that had crept in beneath the door, or around one of the windowpanes. He shuddered a little, clutched his arms to his chest, trying to instil a little warmth there.

"Then," Damon said, "I suppose we can administer the Test."

"The Test?"

Damon's smile returned, a shadow of its former self, and as Mave'c's eyes crept along the monk's clutched hands, he noticed the burn just above his knuckles, a mark which Mave'c hadn't previously noticed . . . or which the monk had hidden from him.

Damon, apparently noticing Mave'c's wandering gaze, slipped his hand back up within the sleeve of his robe. "Tomorrow, at dawn," Damon said, his voice deeper now, somehow, hollowed out almost. "I shall send the boy to wake you."

That same chill lingered in the air now, and Mave'c felt himself shuddering right down to his bones. He had to bite down hard to stop his teeth chattering together, and, without being able to summon another word in his dried-up, and frozen throat, he shuffled on out of the room, giving Damon a parting, sheepish smile.

9

THE NEXT MORNING, tangerine sunlight slunk in through Damon's windowpane and warmed his blankets. But Damon, dazed from a sleepless night, still felt the same ripping cold passing through his whole body, right down to his toes. He was convinced that if he were to so much as move a muscle his toes might break right off.

The fresh winter's air had a stiffness to it this morning, and whenever Damon breathed it into his lungs, it felt like it was scratching him up from the inside. The worst part was when he breathed out, though.

It tasted of ash.

He hauled his blanket up further, right up to his chin. The fabric tickled against his skin, seeming to be rough where before it had been silky smooth. In the near distance he could hear footsteps—what he'd learned to recognise as a monk approaching.

That same *slap* of the sole of a sandal against the stone paving slabs of the corridor.

He turned his head and watched on as the door creaked open, and the younger monk appeared there with that tray that Mave'c had come to see as an integral part of his morning ritual. That woven wicker tray with the steaming broth, and the mug of wild berry tea.

But whereas Mave'c every morning had greeted the boy with a beaming grin, and a hearty Good Morning, this morning he felt hollow—shelled-out, in fact—from his sleepless night.

He felt like a husk of corn able to be blown about by the faintest of breezes.

Mave'c took the tray and slurped down his soup, sucked down

his tea too, while extremely conscious of the boy watching him take his every bite. He caught him looking at him out of the corner of his eye and would've asked him to stop, if he'd only had the strength. Because the truth was that he felt weak—weaker than he'd ever felt in his life, weaker even than bringing in the yield on the longest day of the summer.

Perhaps he was coming down with something. Maybe he could have a message sent to Damon, have someone tell him that he would prefer to take the Test—whatever that was—another day when he was feeling better.

Mave'c even tried to part his lips, to say something to the boy. But he just couldn't. It was like all the air inside his chest had frozen solid. And yet, he still had that burning ashy taste thick in his mouth, almost smothering him.

His hand shook as he laid his emptied mug back down on the wicker tray. And then he met the boy's eye, and knew that he at least had some strength remaining. "I . . . I don't feel . . ."

But he couldn't finish his sentence.

The boy gave him a slight smile and then stooped down to recover the tray. "Yes, we all found it like this, when we were taking the Test."

"I'm . . . I'm . . ." But again Mave'c's throat just swelled up, and he found the words stuck there unsaid.

The boy's quick, blue eyes lingered over his a moment, before looking back off to the door of the room. "I can't say much," he said. "Rules for the Test are that we've gotta keep those taking it pretty much in the dark."

Mave'c watched as the boy's spindly fingers wrapped round the handles of the tray and lifted it into the air with an effortlessness that he felt he would never be able to muster ever again. He watched the boy as he made his way out of the room.

The door shut with a *thunk* behind the boy.

And then, hearing his footsteps slap on their way, along the corridor, Mave'c allowed himself to drop back onto his pillow, and rest there. When he closed his eyes he saw flames licking up his face, and at the same time felt ice clawing through his veins. It was like his body was battling with itself.

MAVE'C SPENT the whole day in bed.

He counted the passing hours by the angle and brightness of the sunlight outside his window. In the afternoon, the sky clouded over, and the sunlight grew dim. And that chill seized hold of him even tighter, as if holding his bunched up in its fist.

He listened hard for any sound off down the corridor, someone bringing him more to eat. But he heard nothing. Only the light stirrings, the quiet shuffling of sandals against stone, somewhere off in the distance of the monastery.

When he breathed in, he heard the air clicking through him, as if nudging its way along his air passages, and into his lungs. Freezing him as it went. When he exhaled, that ashy taste came rolling out of him.

And he knew just what was happening to him, what this *Test* was.

His body *was* doing battle—it was doing battle with fire and ice magic, and trying to stabilise itself in reference to a new normal.

Did he really have to suffer so much to become a monk at Ravensbark?

It was much later, the sky had long turned a midnight blue, when he heard the sound off down the corridor, that familiar *slap* of sandal against stone. And he craned his neck round, his body smoking as it froze to death.

The scene passed in a daze. The figure in the doorway was there, and not there, all at the same time. Of course Mave'c recognised him. Damon. Damon Shriversmyth. But, at the same time, Mave'c's eyesight refused to bring him into focus.

Damon had that same, half-smile fixed on his lips. He held his hands clutched at the tassels of the rope tied round the stomach of his robe. His words took on a floating quality, and the volume of his voice rose and fell, at times almost becoming too loud to stand and at others far too quiet to comprehend. But Mave'c listened to him. To everything he had to say.

"Mave'c? Are you suffering? Are you suffering, Mave'c?"

As Mave'c lay there he felt the ice ripping through his blood, turning his insides cold and useless. It made its way up to his brain too, turning it into nothing more than a pile of slush, useless, numbed slush.

And he felt the flames licking at his toes, rising up his legs. But the flames didn't warm him at all. They gave him no relief from the iciness laying havoc to his guts. They only intensified his pain, made things all the worse.

". . . Mave'c? . . . Mave'c?"

Damon's words again, coming and going. His call to him.

"Mave'c? . . . Mave'c? . . . MAVE'C!"

The final, impossibly-loud call of his name sent reverberations shuddering round the inside of Mave'c's skull, and were so intense as to make him screw up his eyes, ball his fingers into fists, and scream till his tonsils burned.

His tonsils burned from the ice and from the fire, and his body felt like it might rip apart, that his bones might fight their way out through his skin.

"Mave'c? . . . Mave'c? . . . Mave'c?"

The feeling hovered in its place, neither growing worse or getting any better. And Mave'c continued to scream, trying to drown out all other sounds. He beat his fists against his bed, feeling them rebound against the wooden platform below his wiry frame. And he felt the vibrations come back at him.

His heart beat so hard against his ribs that he was afraid it might collude with his bones, and lead a gaolbreak from his body.

His breathing became so shallow that it seemed impossible that his body could be making any sort of use from the action.

And then, slowly, gradually, his mind came back to him.

And then his body.

And he felt the fire and the ice slip away from him.

His skin no longer felt like it was trapping his internal organs.

His heartbeat slowed.

The feeling returned to his toes, to his legs.

And the fierce iciness ripping through him ceased.

Thawed.

Mave'c breathed several times, great heaving, mounting breaths. And when he exhaled the stench and overwhelming taste of ash was gone. He breathed the clean mountain air again. He could smell the stone, the wooden adornments around him, the musky scent of his blanket.

Feeling something akin to delight sweep over him, he turned on his side and faced up to Damon. Mave'c felt the grin pinning his cheeks back, exposing all his crooked teeth, or what remained of them after the fever. Now he had the strength to speak and he was forever grateful. "Did I . . . am I . . . a monk?"

Damon looked long and hard at Mave'c, that same half-smile on his lips, and gave him a gentle shake of the head.

And then Mave'c turned away, contented himself with lying flat on his back, to staring at the ceiling, to the wooden rafters over him, to listening to the furnace crackling somewhere in the distance of his consciousness.

II

F OR SEVERAL MORE WEEKS, Mave'c rested in his room. The Test had really taken all the energy out of his body. As he lay there, in his room, he received his three meals a day from the same young blond monk, and he took his food with mumbled thanks.

Although he never asked, he always hoped that the young monk might say something to him, that he might give him some news on how Mave'c's application to become a monk was coming along. Some days Mave'c wished to see Damon standing there, darkening his doorway, him holding the tray for once. But he never did come.

Mave'c watched the winter evaporate as the first flourish of spring took hold up in the mountains, at Ravensbark. He watched the first green shoots burst through the desolate soil, and the first flower buds grow heavy with dew in the early morning. And the sun rising each day with greater strength than the last.

Mave'c felt his old strength returning—the strength which had seen him through so many bountiful summers—and yet this time it was different.

It *was* different, though he couldn't quite say why.

When he rose in the mornings he would flex his arms up to the ceiling, feel the give and tug of his muscles unknotting, his ageing bones creaking. All those sounds and feelings he was so accustomed to. But there was something else.

Perhaps he was getting old.

Maybe things were worse than he'd imagined.

And he prayed ever day that he would be accepted to stay on here at Ravensbark.

12

W HEN THE DAY DID COME, it was like any other. Mave'c had noted in the long time he'd spent at Ravens-bark, pretty much the whole of the winter, or the darkest part of it at least, that all the days seemed to meld into one.

Here at Ravensbark the whole place just seemed like an eternity, squeezed up here into the mountains, between a pair of peaks. But that was just an illusion. Time *was* trotting on.

He heard those twin pairs of footsteps outside his room, out in the corridor, the sandals slapping stone, and he beat them to the door. This time he yanked it back to expose the corridor. And he couldn't help but feel that smile breaking out on his lips, seeming to ignite his soul.

This might well be the first day of the rest of his life.

There they were: Damon and the young monk. The young monk with Mave'c's breakfast tray, and Damon, his same half-smile still pressed to his lips. Mave'c watched the steam rise off the mug of wild berry tea, and his broth, those flavours that he'd grown to love, to think of as representing *home*.

And now, perhaps, they really would.

Mave'c stood back to usher the two monks into his quarters, and he watched as the younger monk went about laying the wicker tray down, just as he'd watched him do every day for the whole of the winter.

But Mave'c was too excited to eat. He had to know *now*. And so he turned to Damon, looked to him, to that half-smile of his, and waited for what he would say.

Damon's voice was level, controlled, no such hint of that rising and falling intonation back when Mave'c had been stuck in the fever of the Test. "Eat quickly," he said. "You have a long day ahead of you, Mave'c."

Mave'c stood there, stunned for a couple of moments, and then, with a final, grateful glance to the younger monk, he made inroads in his breakfast. He took his broth, and suckled his mug of tea down, and then, finished, he laid everything back down on the tray. And he waited.

Damon's kept up his half-smile, and then beckoned for him to follow, out into the corridor.

Only when Mave'c stood in the doorway did he think to turn and thank the younger monk, but he was hunched over, with his back to him, already gathering up the wicker tray with the emptied bowl and mug.

Well, he could thank him later.

13

DAMON LED MAVE'C through countless winding
corridors, stone on all sides. And Mave'c felt the sleeve of
his tunic brush up against the weeds sticking up through the
cracks, winding their way up to find their place in the sun. He
breathed in the morning air, and his feet felt light, as they should
have, this having been the most relaxing winter of his life.

They descended further through Ravensbark, down and down
again. They emerged out on a lower level which Mave'c had never
before set eyes on: a long, exposed stone path which hung out
from the mountainside.

Down to his right he watched the mountain drop away to a
valley hundreds and hundreds of feet below. He felt his stomach
dip, and his blood froth up. And he quickened his pace to keep up
with Damon as if just thinking about that drop might cause him to
tumble down it.

Damon led him along, his robe fluttering behind him in the
gentle morning breeze, and they re-entered the monastery,
heading into a gloomy opening in its stone façade.

Mave'c sucked in yet more air as he followed the Abbot.

Back inside the monastery building, back among the cool
stone, and the light, fresh air, Mave'c caught a whiff of the overpowering smell of horses. He looked about him and realised that
they'd come down into a stable. Every day in Ravensbark
surprised him. He kept discovering new nooks and crannies all
over the place.

Damon continued to walk along, treading the straw-covered
floor, his robe still sweeping at his ankles. Stable doors lined either
side of the path. And, deeper within, the horses rose up from their
reclining postures, as if anticipating getting fed.

Mave'c jogged to keep up the pace, and looked in on some of the horses. He took in their long noses, their black, shining eyes, and their strong jaws, barely concealed within their hairy muzzles.

They arrived out the other side of the stables, into a larger room, with a domed roof.

Mave'c peered up to the rafters above them, and sucked in the deep woody smell all around. There was all manner of tack for horses hanging off hooks. Chains and leather. Riding boots, and crops. And then, he saw just where Damon was heading over to.

To the rack which held the riding cloaks.

Mave'c felt a chill descend over him. He knew what he was bound for now. That his dreams of staying here in Ravensbark were forever dashed. He watched as Damon reached up for one of the cloaks, took in that distinctive, off-brown colour of the cloak, and another shudder ran up his spine.

Damon brought the elected cloak down from its hook and turned to Mave'c. Now there was no smile on his lips, nor the suggestion that he had *ever* smiled in his life. A sombre shadow seemed to fall across his face, and his cheeks which had seemed bulbous and bright with colour when Mave'c had first met him, now just seemed dingy and grey.

Numbness draped over Mave'c as he stood there, just an observer, as Damon laid the cloak around Mave'c's shoulders, and Mave'c felt the material cling to his frame, hug him in that way he'd seen the cloak hug the others. The others he'd seen.

The *hobblesmen.*

That was what he was now. He was a man without a home. Condemned to drift about the world, trudging from one place to the next, jabbering away inanely, the hood of his cloak darkening his face, stopping anyone from reading his expression.

He would *never* be a monk.

Mave'c felt his lip trembling just a little, but he managed to speak. "Wha . . . what happened? Did . . . did I do something, something wrong?"

Damon stood back and eyed him for a long while, as if pausing to ensure that the cloak was a perfect fit.

But Mave'c knew there was no need for that caution, because thinking to himself, really burrowing down inside his soul, he knew that *he* could never have become a monk.

And then Damon said, "You've still got magic stirring in your veins, as you will do until the day you die. The Test showed that you cannot exist between ice and fire, they would simply break you in two between them."

Then Damon smiled faintly. "It's a mercy to let you go—if I'd allowed you to spend any longer in the thralls of the ice and fire magic they would've destroyed you, ripped you apart from the inside-out. Now, at least, you can have something of a life. But you shall never be a monk."

Mave'c nodded, although he wished that crying out might do some good. But he knew that there was nothing he could do, any more than he could rip out his own soul, and replace it with another.

"But you can never settle," Damon continued. "You must stay distant from other people, or you shall bring your own curse to bear on them."

Again, Mave'c nodded. He knew what was at stake, and what his responsibility, as a hobblesman, was now.

He looked back to Damon.

Damon reached out and rested his hand on Mave'c's shoulder, and gave it a strong squeeze. Another of those half-smiles of his, and then he added, "Then all I have to say to you is good luck," and with that he let go of Mave'c and stood back.

Mave'c stared into Damon's eyes for the last time, and then, looking out to the clean mountain air opening up before him, the strong, azure sky ahead, and the sun rising up over the snowy peaks like the glint off a scythe, he put one foot in front of the other.

One after the other.

And he was gone.

Just another hobblesman to walk the world forever more.

DAWN'S SIREN

HILDIE LAY on her back and felt for the pail of water down by her side. She dipped her fingers into it. The water was still warm. She brought her fingers back out and sucked the moisture off. That felt good, took the dryness out of her mouth. Did something to calm the hunger in her belly.

Just outside the canvas of their tent, she could hear the snowflakes rustling as they landed on the leaves in the trees. Somewhere in the undergrowth, a few paces from where she laid her head, she could hear something scuttling along. A mouse, or a rat, perhaps.

She remembered, a long while ago now, when they'd stayed in a village, she'd gone to school. And one day, just when they'd been coming to the end of a lesson, a rat had scurried out from somewhere in the wall.

All the girls in the class had screamed.

Their piercing screams still seemed to reverberate about her head.

And the boys had all leapt from their seats and tried to stomp the rat dead.

And one of them had succeeded.

Hildie remembered that she'd simply sat down, in her seat, not really doing much of anything, just watching the children. Surprised at how they were acting. Because it'd never occurred to her to be afraid of something so small as a rat.

She breathed in deep and felt the musky odour linger in her nostrils, before she took it down into her lungs, made it a part of herself.

Over, on the other side of the tent, she could see the forms of her mother and father. Both of them sleeping. Entwined, one around the other. Their shoulders rose and fell with their breathing. As she looked down at them, down to her father's hands, she saw that ember glow at his fingertips, those fire fingers, as she named them. And she knew that his same fire blood was inside her. That, just like him, she would grow up to be a fire mage.

She listened harder for that scuttling creature, close by to her ear. She allowed her imagination to go wild. Thought about just what it might be. Sure, it could be a rat, but what if it was a boar . . . or a deer?

Perhaps it might be some magical creature, something undocumented. Although her father had told her that really wasn't likely, not here in the Kingdom of Shellacnass. Long ago they'd chased the magic away—into neighbouring kingdoms, underground, into mountain pits, into the twilight.

And that was just what had happened to them, her family, too. They'd been chased away with the rest of it, condemned to this life of forever running away.

Somewhere in the distance, a twig snapped.

A shiver ran through Hildie's veins, and she sat up straight, cocked her ears in the direction of the sound. After all their travelling through the kingdom, all this running away, she'd learned that she had to pay attention to everything. Any detail that might reveal someone after them.

She glanced over at her parents and, seeing them sleeping on, felt somewhat assured. Her father had something of a sense for danger and would often be the one to rouse them. It was probably nothing. But she might as well go check.

On her hands and knees, she crawled her way along the floor of the tent, and over to the opening. She untoggled the wooden fastening, and glanced out through the narrow gap.

The sun was just rising through the wood, only beginning to shine through the countless trunks, to illuminate the thick undergrowth, and to reflect off the dew-soaked ground, dazzling Hildie with the strength of its light.

She cocked her head to one side and listened carefully. She remembered just what her father had always taught her about breathing, that she had to make her breaths as regular, and as quiet as she could manage if she hoped to hear anything of value. And that was what she did now.

Beneath her knees, and through the ground cloth of the tent, she felt the knobbly remnants of tree roots poking through. But she ignored the discomfort, and just concentrated on listening.

Another *snap* followed by the rustling of leaves.

And then a low rumble of chatter.

People.

She was certain.

Hildie swivelled round and hissed at her parents, again in the way that her father had taught her, so that she would be mistaken for a wild animal by anyone listening in. And she watched her father slowly stir from his place, and those emerald green eyes that were the same as her own glimmer back at her through the half-light of the tent.

He took her in, and then stiffened.

Hildie could tell that he'd heard them too.

He held still, and Hildie mimicked him, afraid that she might be the one to give them away. When he spoke it was in a whisper. "At least a dozen of them," he said, then tilted his head a little to the side. "No, *more*."

Hildie felt the air in her body go cold, and that rumble of warmth start up in her belly. That was one of those feelings that she'd learned to recognise—with her father's guidance—as the stirring of the fire magic within her. And she knew that it was a combination of rage, of fury, and a fierce protective instinct for her family. She knew that her father felt the same, and wondered how much impossibly stronger it would be within *him*.

He met her eye in the gloom, and said, his voice still level, plain-speaking and calm, "They're headed right for us."

Hildie's heart hammered up into her throat, and she felt her chest tighten. That fire in her gut just got hotter and hotter, and she could almost swear that she felt flames licking at her throat. But she stayed where she was, looked to her father. "What do we do?"

Her father nudged her mother awake, and she came to with a slight smile on her lips, her lids only just parted. "Come on," he said. "We have to get up. We have to get away."

Hildie packed up her own belongings, working quickly to get all of her few things gathered together, her clothes and her bedding. And then she helped her father to take down the canvas tent, to roll it back up and help him strap it to the rest of their luggage they would carry with them.

And then, with everything ready to go, Hildie heard, coming from the trees, in a distinct, gravelly drawl that she recognised as the dialect from Ilsnare—the Crystal City, "Stay right where you are or I'll have you shot."

2

HILDIE FROZE where she was, and she looked to her mother and father's faces, saw their wide-eyed expressions, their parted lips, and she knew that they were in trouble, that they had been cornered by these men . . . men who wanted them dead.

And then she watched as her father's expression transformed, from wide-eyed shock, to one of uneasy enquiry. "Oh?" he said, with a slight hop in his voice that Hildie had never heard before. "Is there some trouble?"

There was a long pause from the hidden men, before the same voice replied, "Don't you play games with me, *mage*. I can *smell* the magic on you—on *all* of you." Another pause, and perhaps a muttered order to one of his men. "If you so much as move from where you stand, I'll have a crossbow bolt fired straight through your heart."

Hildie looked to her father, feeling her pulse throbbing in her cheeks. Sweat dampened her tunic now, despite the fresh morning air, and the light smells of the forest, that ever-green scent that seemed to hang over everything, seemed to smother her now.

Her father just stayed still. He looked more under control, his brow furrowed as he silently plotted their next move. Sometimes she wondered whether other young girls thought about their father as a hero—but she knew that her father was really special, that he had powers that other fathers could only dream of.

"Mage," the voice from the woods said, "I'm sending in my men to have you put into chains. Just stay right where you are, and you might survive the trip to the gaol."

Hildie listened to the boots trudging through the undergrowth, the snapping of twigs a cacophony now, and several stones were kicked off over the soft ground, sent tumbling along until they lost momentum or collided with a sturdy tree trunk.

And then the men appeared from between the trees.

They all wore the light grey uniforms of the Ilsnare Royal Guards. She had learned to recognise her enemy during their whole time on the run, and she knew enough of them to smell the danger that clung to them. Whenever her father spoke about them he did so with a spit or an uttered swearword. And so she'd learned to despise them just as her father did.

Just like her father had said, the guards swarmed all around them, several more than a dozen, and from all directions. It was clear to Hildie now that they'd planned this well, that they'd had them surrounded. They'd never had a chance.

The guards all had scimitars, held down at their thighs. But, from what Hildie had seen of her father's powers, she knew they'd need much more than just scimitars if they were going to provide any real sort of resistance.

The guards just kept coming out from the trees. She heard the jangling of chains, and Hildie watched on as a pair of guards emerged from the trees behind, and approached her mother and father, before clasping chains around their wrists and ankles, their necks.

Then she felt a couple of pairs of hands on her, and the chill of the steel against her own skin. That *snap* as the mechanism locked into place, and then the jangle of the chains as they settled themselves around their victim.

With them all chained, the guards all stood back, raising their scimitars and standing with straight backs, their gaze looking up through the trees, to the emerging sky above.

Hildie heard the trudge of yet more footsteps, and she looked through the parted leaves to see a man walk into the clearing.

He had a square chin, and hefty shoulders. Fair hair. And he looked much younger than Hildie would've supposed from his voice. His expression was stern, and his eyes drawn back, almost sunken, in their sockets. She turned to look at his side, to the sword that hung from his hip. Its hilt glinted dully in the dim sunlight that penetrated the canopy of the forest.

The man had no interest in Hildie, he trudged right up to her father, and fixed him with a pout, a slight sneer. "Ma'reygar, I presume."

A tingle ran up Hildie's spine. She wasn't used to people recognising her father. Not this soon. The reason they kept on travelling all the time was so that people wouldn't place him, *any* of them. And yet this man, this member of the Royal Guards, had identified him right away.

Hildie's father just smiled gently. "And you are?"

"Herimyre, Captain of the Royal Guards."

Hildie's father snorted a laugh, and Hildie felt a tremble in her gut. She always got afraid when her father acted like this, as if somehow the situation was amusing. She knew that this was when people got hurt. And there were lots of men surrounding them. Lots of people *to* get hurt.

"Nah," Hildie's father said. "I don't believe you. Numwhip is Captain of the Royal Guards."

"Not anymore, he's not," Herimyre said. "Killed in the Sable Mountains. Brains dashed to pieces by trolls."

Hildie's gut clenched at hearing that. Although she'd never met a troll, or any other sort of magical creature—she'd never even been outside the Kingdom of Shellacnass—she could picture the image in her mind. And it terrified her.

"Guess that's not too bad for your own career, then?" Hildie's father replied.

This raised a slight smirk from Herimyre. "My only duty is to serve my king, and to keep the people of Shellacnass safe."

3

HILDIE WATCHED her father closely as the guards urged them all forwards with their scimitars. She looked to her mother's face, but her mother had her eyes fixed to the toes of her shoes. Her father stayed still a couple of seconds before one of the guards poked him in the back with the tip of his scimitar. And then, just as he shuffled forwards, he glanced back over his shoulder to Hildie.

Hildie felt a tremor in her gut—she could see the fire in his eyes, beyond the emerald-green, buried there, always threatening to bounce out, to escape. And she felt the tip of the scimitar in her own back and started walking.

She trudged onwards, listening to the crunch of the guards' boots on the crispy, iced-over forest floor. She overheard her father speaking with Herimyre, the Captain of the Guards. It was just like her father to speak like that, to keep jabbering on. She knew that it was simply an act, a way to make his enemies think that he was a stupid blabber-mouth. It was just what he did as he bade his time in making his move.

She stared forwards, watching the backs of her parents' heads as they swaggered on their way. She saw her father continuing to speak with Herimyre, but she couldn't hear his words. She supposed he was riling him even more about the circumstances under which he'd been appointed Captain of the Royal Guards.

Her father always said that working for the king was like cutting your neighbour's throat.

She guessed they'd been walking for about half an hour, perhaps as much as an hour, when they reached the fringes of the forest. She looked about her at the thinning trees, and the expanse of the plains opening up before them. Those plains, they were what spelled danger. And she had to take great care. All their lives they'd avoided the plains.

Now, though, those plains were a frozen expanse, snow piled up over the long grass, and when the wind blew its way across the plains she felt the sting of its chill on her cheeks, her mouth drying up and her nostrils shrivelling with its harsh scent.

The plains rolled away for miles and miles with only the odd tree, dusted in snow, to give any sense of proportion. In the foreground she saw the guards' camp, the collection of twenty or so tents, and their horses all tied up, munching their way through the grass they'd exposed from beneath the snow by shuffling their noses through it.

The sun just about tilted up above the horizon, shedding its first rays over the plains, and giving a little warmth to the otherwise frozen expanse. It warmed Hildie's blood—somehow seemed to build up her confidence, make her feel better about the situation.

As she followed on her father's heels, her eyes fixed on the nape of her father's neck, she listened to her chains clinking, and the breathing of the guards right behind her. She wished she could do something—*anything*—to help save her family. And she felt that warmth stirring in her belly again. But she had to patient. It wouldn't do for her to get carried away. That might put an end to whatever masterstroke it was that her father was planning.

Led by Herimyre, they spiralled down the gentle slope to the camp. Hildie kept her eyes on her father at all times, and felt her blood surging round her cheeks, tasted its rustiness in her mouth. Her heart beat against her ribs.

Herimyre barked an order out in the Ilsnare dialect, something that Hildie didn't understand, and all the guards brought them to a halt. They lined up Hildie, her mother and father all in a row, side by side. When Hildie tilted her head to one side, to glance to her father, Herimyre barked out something else to her.

She had no need to understand his words to know that she wasn't to look anywhere but the space in front of her nose.

She watched on as, in the background, the guards worked to harness horses, to bring them round from their feeding on the grass beneath the snow. The horses tossed their heads, and shook manes as the guards brought them forwards. And then Hildie saw the cart as it appeared from round the back of one of the tents. It was just like the ones she'd always seen.

A prison cart.

Its bars were thick steel, grey and unfeeling. The wood was beaten-up and weathered, all chipped and chapped. Hildie felt more of a shudder pass round the collar of her tunic from looking at the prison cart than from the stiff northern wind now blowing across the plains.

She glanced to her father, and received another reprimand from Herimyre.

The cart trundled towards them, led for the time being by two of the guards. Its wheels bounced over the uneven, frozen ground, and the guards' breath clouded before their faces. They brought the cart to a rest before Hildie and her family. Then one of the guards undid the catch to the barred door which led onto the cart and stood to attention beside it, ready for whatever order Herimyre deigned to give.

Hildie first felt it grow deep within her, that unmistakable rising heat. This time, though, she knew that it wasn't coming from herself, but from her father. She had no need to look to him to know that. When she looked over the faces of the guards, she knew that they had failed to notice what she had. But, when she chanced a look to Herimyre, saw his widened eyes, his flaring nostrils, she knew that when he'd said that he could smell magic that he wasn't lying. And he was so sure of what was now happening not to notice that Hildie now stared right at him, rather than into the space before her.

The inferno began when that first strand of sunlight hit Hildie's cheek.

4

FLAMES DANCED all around them, seemed to rush right out from Hildie. She closed her eyes tight and channelled it, or at least tried. She could feel the power, like a rushing torrent of water, and knew that she had neither the ability nor the natural strength to control it. It just passed through her . . . or out of her?

She clasped her eyes shut as she listened to the screams of the guards as the flames roasted them. The stench of burning human skin, reminding Hildie of rotten pork roasting on an open fire. All the hairs on her body stood on end, and she tasted that ash in her mouth, at the back of her throat. Her heart pounded at her temples with the mightiest migraine she'd ever had in her life.

The screams continued, the horses whinnied, and screeched, and she smelled the sour stench of horsemeat among everything else. The stench of it wrapped over her nostrils and mouth, entered her lungs and seeped into her blood, part of her forever more.

And then, as the flames seemed to abate, and the heat lessened, and her heart began to resume its normal rhythms, she opened her eyes.

The snow all around them had melted. Of course it had. How could it have resisted the stifling heat of it all? And the grass the flames had exposed was singed where it wasn't completely devoured, and replaced with mounted earth.

She turned her head, looked around her.

Dead bodies. Roasted. Prostrate.

And they were scattered all around her. Their mouths hanging open in shock, their eyeballs just charred sockets. Their flesh like tanned hide.

She breathed in. Then again. Her heart hammered harder. Had she done this? Had the fire magic come from within her?

Her focus moved to the cart. Now it was only cinders. The wood just ashes on the burned ground. And that made her glad— they wouldn't take her prisoner today.

Then, feeling the daze flutter away from her mind, allowing her logical thoughts to take over, she looked round to where her father stood.

Her father, Ma'reygar—the feared fire mage—stood there, his fists crunched up down at his sides, his expression glowering. But not at Hildie, nor at the dozens of dead bodies. All around.

He was glowering at Herimyre.

5

HILDIE FELT her chest tighten and her breath stick in her throat. Looking around she knew that all the other guards were dead—had been roasted by her father's spell. And yet Herimyre still stood there. It took her another couple of seconds to realise just how he'd managed it, to absorb the details. And then she did.

Herimyre stood holding Hildie's mother, his arm wrapped tight around her throat, pinning her in position from his place at her back. He held the blade of his sword just beneath her chin. His eyes were wild, his hair stirred up, slightly charred. But other than that it seemed that Hildie's father's spell had had no impact whatsoever upon him.

And then Hildie took a little longer to take in the sword—saw that the blade, ever so slightly, was glowing a faint orange colour, the colour of the sun's rays as they licked at the horizon. And she turned to her father, looking for some explanation.

But, of course, he only had eyes for Herimyre.

Hildie's father's voice seemed to come from the very base of his lungs, from some obsidian pit within himself. "Let. Her. Go."

Herimyre retained his smirk, the sword not so much as shaking in his grip as he held it in place at Hildie's mother's throat. He made no move to reply either.

Hildie's father flared his eyes, and raised his hands. Hildie saw the glimmer of flames there, growing at his fingertips, threatening to burst right out. She thought this man, this *Herimyre*, completely mad. What was he trying to prove here? First he'd somehow miraculously escaped her father's spell and now he was taking a stand.

. . . And if she knew anything at all of her father she was sure it was likely to be a last stand.

Just as her father raised his hands above his head, and she saw the sparks begin to surge out from his fingertips, she heard Herimyre's voice rise above all else, and stop her father before he had a chance to cast the spell.

"I see you've not much experience with magical relics."

Hildie's father kept up his posture, those flames still threatening to burst from his fingers at any second, and yet he held back. Waited to see just what this guard had to say.

Hildie felt her whole body go numb, and her muscles lock up. She ground her teeth with anger, just like her father, demanding inside her mind that Herimyre let her mother go.

Hildie's father looked to him again. "What do you mean?"

Herimyre's smirk got wider still. He nodded to his sword, still held to Hildie's mother's throat, and still glowing that faint tone of orange. "Tysron. You've never heard of it?"

Hildie studied her father's face in profile, saw the slight tightening of the wrinkles around his eyes, and she knew that he had heard of it, that he had just now realised what it was that he faced. Hildie stared on, determined to remain resilient.

Hildie's father drew a quick breath, but kept his hands raised. "I wondered how you managed to survive Dawn's Siren."

Hildie supposed that Dawn's Siren was the spell, that mighty spell, her father had cast.

Herimyre grinned now, and the blade of the sword was losing its orange sheen. "Anything you try to hit me with I can well take care of." He glanced back over his shoulder briefly, to the burned-out campsite, and then to a single horse which stood about a hundred paces away, kicking its feet and throwing its head.

Now Hildie could hear its winnowing carrying on the wind. She supposed that Herimyre had prepared for this, that he had taken precautions on approaching the great Ma'reygar. And he had the advantage here, of that there was no question.

"So," Herimyre said. "How about we strike a deal. If you'll come quietly with me, Ma'reygar, then I'll be prepared to see that your wife and daughter are taken care of when we return to Ilsnare."

"You mean you'll torture them before you kill them?" Hildie's father said, his voice a growl.

"Do you think so little of my promises?"

"I know what mortals are like."

Herimyre shrugged, still keeping the edge of the blade at Hildie's mother's chin.

Hildie stared into her mother's eyes, saw the slight film over them, the tears threatening to burst from the surface at any second. She tried to speak to her through her mind—to tell her to be brave, to wait there, and be patient. Hildie was certain that her father could still beat Herimyre, whatever it took.

Hildie looked to her father to see what he might do.

Hildie's father kept his hands raised, those flames still tickling all over his palms, occasionally flaring out from his fingertips. And then, with a single, swift turn of the head, he looked in Hildie's direction, gave her a doleful and heavy nod.

And Hildie knew just what she was to do.

She took a step forward and entered her father's fiery glow and, together, they channelled all their magic into a ball and hurled it at Herimyre.

6

AN ALMIGHTY *thwack* resounded through the air. It reminded Hildie of when they'd been up to the Sable Mountains, where they'd hidden out one summer, and how on one stormy night, while they camped on the cusp of a valley, she heard a thunderbolt jack into the hillside. The sound it had made as it had hit the solid rock was just the same sound that her and her father's combined magic made now.

It knocked her backwards, and she hit the ground several paces behind. She felt herself fall onto the scorched dirt, and a tingle of pain shot up from her lower back, and danced between her shoulder blades. For a few seconds she was dazed, completely thrown off her bearings. Rubbing her head, she looked about her.

Her father was close by, a few paces from her, and up ahead she saw the great orb, the glow of flame that formed round Herimyre and Hildie's mother. Hildie observed the sword, saw it glowing fire-orange now.

Herimyre backed away from them, still surrounded by that orb, still with his sword at her mother's chin, gradually making his way to the horse which stood tethered up a safe distance from the carnage which had unfolded this morning.

Hildie studied her father, saw that he had a rivulet of blood running down from his temple. His chest rose and fell rapidly, and sweat slithered down his cheeks. She looked again to Herimyre, still retreating, but she knew that it was over now. That there was nothing she or her father could do. She'd heard her father speak about the damage a deflected spell could do to the mage that had cast it, and that familiar panic she'd felt at putting herself into that mage's shoes returned to her in a flurry.

Often it meant death.

Her temples still pounding and feeling the residues of the fire still kindling within her, she crawled over to where her father lay, and rested her hand over his forehead. And she whipped it back just as quickly, feeling it burn against her own skin.

She waited another few tentative moments, and then reached down to feel for her father's pulse. She had expected it to be weak, barely present, but instead it was impossibly fast, bouncing along far quicker than she could ever possibly count. And before long she had to whip her hand back from him again, from the searing heat there.

She looked off into the distance, to see that Herimyre had arrived at his waiting horse's side now, and that he still had hold of her mother. She wondered whether he would return to them, if he would come over to finish her father . . . and her, off. But she just watched on as he mounted the horse, and then kicked it into a gallop. Her mother sitting in front of him, gripping hold of the mane, her eyes wide and twinkling even from this distance.

After watching the horse gallop off over the horizon and out of sight, she felt tears rise in her eyes, and only with the greatest of force did she manage to suppress them, to push them right back down.

She turned back to look at her father, shaking her head and unable to keep the sobs out of her voice. "Why didn't he come back for us?" she said.

Her father's face was a light shade of charcoal, his lips crimson. Although his eyes remained firmly sealed, and his features other-wise grey, he managed to speak. "He doesn't . . . want to trap me, *us*," he said. "He . . . he wants a war."

"A war?"

Her father could only nod vaguely.

Hildie frowned, feeling the wrinkles engrave themselves deep into her forehead, the wrinkles themselves felt like iron nails embedding themselves in her skull, worsening her migraine. "But, how is he going to have a war by taking Mother?"

Her father made no reply.

And then Hildie thought that she understood—that she'd caught a grip on just what was going on, what her father was thinking in his mind.

She felt herself cool, the fire magic loosen its hold on her just for a few seconds, and her migraine lessen. "You're going to save her, aren't you?"

Her father, crushing his eyelids tight, just nodded to her.

"And if she can't be saved then he'll have his war?"

Again, her father nodded.

Hildie drew a long breath, feeling that familiar chill returning to the air, and with it carrying the taint of all those burned-up corpses, lying not so far away from them, and then she looked off to the horizon, to the sun, and saw it twinkling its golden rays over everything—over the snow which covered the plains.

And she knew that Herimyre would have his fight—that he had stirred up the fire, and the ice, and that, just like her father, she wouldn't rest till he had been brought to justice.

Till some sense of balance had returned to the world.

THE THREADED PIT

IN THE DISTANCE Xeda could hear the snickering of the sea breeze. It rattled its way in through the mouth of the cave—a mile away from here, all told—and then through the endless tunnels of this place, the Threaded Pit, and would have chilled any less of a man than he was.

He could smell the thick salt that carried on its breath, and it clambered in through his nostrils, and sent a tingle through his tongue. That was what passed for the outside world down here, in this pit. The only detail that caught up with him down here in this gloomy, swirling obsidian.

Sometimes he wondered whether he'd lost his mind, and that was when he wondered whether he'd ever had it in the first place. Had he ever? Certainly, having a good, solid presence of mind might've stopped him ending up here, in this predicament he found himself.

Too weak for sunlight.

Fire a branding iron against his skin.

Warmth his bitter enemy.

No, the damp down here, the ever-clawing chill of this place, those were his allies—though they were more than simple allies now. They were part of him. Part of his blood and skin, just as much his body as the dank rocks he rested up against, that served as his furniture, and which were his only company down here.

As he sniffed at the sea breeze, he could hear it howling further off down the tunnel. Instinctively, he knew what it was, that it was a storm, nothing else it could be. If he listened hard, if he tuned his thoughts out just so, he could hear the lashing of the wind against the waves and the *crash* as the water beating up against the rocks.

And that fine ocean spray floated its way on that bitter wind, driving it around the tunnels, and then to Xeda, sat right here, and waiting.

Waiting for what?

For light, for dark?

Death, life?

Perhaps he was waiting for everything. Just *something*, something which would permit him to walk the world again like a mortal, not as the frail, shell of a person—though was he a person any longer?—that he'd become.

As he sank back up against the rock, felt its familiar jagged points point themselves into his leathered, scarred-up flesh, he thought of that battle as he did every day. It seemed so long ago now, such a long time ago. And yet it still plagued his mind every day, because he had to live with its consequences always.

He would be *forever* living with the consequences.

The fire had done for him, of that he was certain. If it hadn't been for the fire, well, things would've been totally different. He would still have his power. Those magical artefacts would still be his, and he might—just *might*—be the leader of the world.

Not the magical world, nor even simply the mortal world, but the whole of it might be his.

But his was the burden of the would-be hero—the *beaten* hero —although he knew that many more people might well see him as a monster. Weak mortals and mages. Those that could not see beyond the tips of their own noses, the ones that he had grown to despise, and curse late into the equally bleak days and nights down here in the Threaded Pit.

Only tonight was different from other nights, yes, he could smell it now. That *smell* hanging on the air, rushing in from the mouth of the cave. That rusty stench, that *stench* he'd grown so acquainted with, the one that he wasn't sure whether or not to think of as a foe or a friend, because on its tide rode the promise of power.

Absolute power.

And that promise was all that kept him alive, all things considered.

And that promise was blood.

2

XEDA shifted his raggedy feet off the rock and dropped down onto the cool earth floor. He adjusted the bandages wrapped about his feet, the ones that had become so mottled and bunged-up with blood that they might as well have been skin.

In many ways those bandages *were* now his skin.

And he shifted through the ever-deepening shadows, through the rich and stodgy gloom, his nose leading him along the trail, tantalising, and tugging at his senses, like the tickle of a finger to his smashed and melted and cobbled-together chin.

Blood.

And blood again.

He could feel the *throb* of it passing through his veins, of that magic lost to him long ago, and which still lurked in his veins. The magic which had betrayed him many times over, and had left him here in this truly wretched shape.

And yet, that same magic, might it take him back now if he could only find a way?

Though pain was a long-forgotten sensation to Xeda, he could feel a dull prickling sensation passing across the soles of his feet. He had been sat down at that rock for so long—how long? . . . A day? A few days? A week? Months?

Time meant nothing.

But now he felt it pushing him forwards, all his senses being restored to him, and the promise of that blood, that throbbing and utterly virile scent. The one which could keep him from the jaws of Death for a little longer, or so it seemed to promise.

The lashing of the waves filled Xeda's ears, and the salty scent of the sea continued to coil its way up his nostrils, and that tickling finger at his chin only enticed him further—*harder*—and who was he not to obey?

He had obeyed his whole life.

Obeying had got him here.

And while it might not be much, it was all he could count on.

He switched and swathed himself in the darkness, using it as a veil . . . just as much as he used the cloak which he wore, the only piece of magic that he had left, the only scrap of material that kept the spectre of Death truly away.

3

WHEN XEDA COULD SENSE the blood so close and thick in his nostrils that it was all he could do to keep his body under control, to stop it trembling with anticipation, he skulked back in the gloom and eyed the path up ahead.

The moonlight which streamed in through the mouth of the cave.

Sunlight would've been a different matter, but moonlight . . . that he could cope with.

He sniffed half a dozen times at the air, still unsure whether or not to trust his sense of smell, but what else did he have? He had been living down here, in this irrepressible darkness for so long now, trusting that scent to catch his dinner—to squash rats up against the rocks with the flat of his hand and feast on them, suck them clean of their last entrails.

Blood.

It still resounded through his mouth with a sharp tang, and excited his breathing. He had to calm himself, had to slow his heart from racing ahead of him, because he had to leave his prey unaware.

He had to leave his prey unknowing.

He listened to the howling of the wind, and felt the frosting of the sea foam layering onto his cheeks, smothering him in its saltiness, that stench of the sea that had been the bane of his existence for so long. Almost like hope at the end of the tunnel. And it tempted him, whipped him up into a frenzy. And then it dropped him.

The moonlight shod its inadequate light onto the mouth of the cave, and he watched the figure slinking through the shadows, almost as weary and careful as he was himself. But why wouldn't he be? He was a stranger here, and he had to take care.

Now that the moon shone a little on the stranger, set him in profile, Xeda could make out the rags that hung off him. Almost like the rags which Xeda wore, all things considered, excepting of course the cloak that clung to Xeda's frame, the one which, among other things, allowed him to slip into the darkness.

Be almost totally unseen.

The stranger's boots crunched on the millions of shells which lined the entrance to the cave, that sound which Xeda had waited so long to hear. Not since his master had come to visit him, years ago now—or decades, perhaps?—had he heard that sound. Nothing larger than the *pitter-patter* of rat's paws.

In comparison, this stranger's steps were like claps of thunder.

And they seemed to squeeze Xeda's heart, to set it pumping all the more vigorously, sending blood pulsing to his temples, and making him crazy for this stranger.

He watched the stranger's breath come out of his mouth in clouds, and watched carefully as he laid his hands on the rocks he passed by to steady himself, to keep himself upright.

Xeda knew that there was no way out of this cave, he had surely looked for long enough, and this man would've been better turning round, making a swim against the almighty tides, trying to make his way about the headland.

But how should the stranger know?

Who should have told *him*?

Xeda's breaths came like whispers now, and he felt them chill and sting his throat, as he took in that freezing air, the air cast off from the sea. And he could still hear the crashing of the waves, the constant dig as the waves snatched up the pebbles lining the beach before bringing them down with mind-numbing power and elegance.

Or, at least, from what he remembered of waves' power he gathered that, because he hadn't dared set foot out onto the beach for years now.

Not for years.

The stranger continued his prowl, his boots unknowingly stirring up the mounted up shells and pebbles, and causing them to clatter one against the other. Creating a cacophony which Xeda was totally sure rang right through the Threaded Pit, through its labyrinthine tunnels, surely all the way back to where Xeda made his bed.

And then, all of a sudden, the stranger came to a stop. Seemed to peer right at Xeda. Or, right *through* him, as the case might've been.

And Xeda regarded the man.

4

A SAILOR, that much was certain from the start. And a *shipwrecked* sailor at that. His clothing hung down him in rags. Though the moonlight was dim, half concealed by the clouds which blew about on the crest of the storm, it was near enough blinding for Xeda.

Xeda could make out the sailor's fair hair, his scrappy beard, and his emaciated frame. He could've done with a little more meat on him, but what had Xeda expected from a sailor? Shouldn't he just be happy to have someone down here with him, someone to *share* with him? Some *fresh* meat?

"Hello?" the sailor said.

Xeda analysed the voice. It'd been a long time since he'd heard a *voice*, why not since his mas—

"Is someone there?" the sailor said.

Xeda slunk back, further into the shadows, keeping his cloak well fitted to his body, close to his skin, knowing that he must remain hidden from the stranger at all costs—until there was no other option.

Until the moment of *death*.

The sailor screwed up his eyes, clearly unaccustomed to the over-riding gloom which dominated the cave, and then he looked back over his shoulder, back to sea.

Good, that was good. If he would run, Xeda would let him go. Sure enough he would wash himself up on the beach sooner or later, and Xeda would have his feast then. He would drag him into the darkness of the Threaded Pit all the same . . . though without the squirming.

"I . . . I . . ." the sailor said, but could not finish.

He muttered something to himself, which Xeda recalled as

being the first sign of madness. Sure, he had been down here a long while, down here in the Threaded Pit, but at least he wasn't speaking to himself. Not that he'd noticed, anyway.

The sailor continued to glare off into the darkness, now looking away from Xeda, not even looking through him any longer. And Xeda could see the hunger reflected in the man's eyes, and then, as the moonlight caught the man's body, he saw just what had drawn him here, to the mouth of the cave.

That hunk of flesh, all battered and bloody, and leaking out from him.

And the blood, that sweet, rusty smell which gouged through the air and made Xeda's stomach rumble, his heart turn in his chest. He wished for it. Felt the deep and irrepressible urge for it, and he wanted it more than anything he'd ever wanted.

Wanted it more than his freedom.

More than *escape*.

The man was wounded, wounded in a shipwreck, Xeda supposed.

As if to confirm this, Xeda looked off past the man, back out to sea, to the curling waves, to the thrashing tides, and tried to see just where this man had come from. Where this . . . this *gift* had come from.

But no, there was nothing out there. Not for Xeda. He would just have to content himself with imagination, and with the knowledge that this man would be his only catch. If he could catch him at all.

Condensation dripped down from the mouth of the cave.

Drip. Drip. Drip.

The man cocked his head backwards, and looked to the sound, and Xeda made his move, springing out from the darkness, and towards the man all at once.

But the man, despite his weariness, was quick, and thought to step to one side before Xeda could catch him with his hand, with those fingernails which had long ago warped into something else. Into what might've been described as *claws*.

The man panted hard, stepped back—took one too many steps back, and then tumbled over on his backside. The moonlight showered over his face, and he looked up above him with rounded and desperate eyes, the slight glean off them giving away the tears which lurked just below the surface. "Please," the man said. "Please. I ... I ..."

Xeda caught the man in his glare, and felt himself holding back. Though the blood was still fresh in his nostrils, and almost overpowering all other senses, and his mouth awash with saliva— with *anticipation*—he held himself back.

It was as if an invisible arm held him back. Stopped him going any further. Yes, before he had had a name for that invisible arm, for that restraining influence within himself.

He had called it *mortal*.

5

THE MAN QUIVERED HARD, and soon Xeda could scent the sweat mixed with the salt of the sea and, a little further off, like a neat little *twist*, the stench of urine, all smudged into the man's clothes. What weak and pitiful creatures men became in these circumstances, when out in the dark, and all alone.

Just leather pouches of rotten water, were they anything more?

"Please," the man said, and he fumbled at his ragged waistcoat, for a pocket snuggled away within, and he withdrew a purse.

Xeda heard the *tinkle* of change within it, and he saw how sodden that purse had grown, how it had once been a fine material—*velvet*, perhaps—but now it was thoroughly ruined.

Irretrievably ruined.

Unabated, the man unravelled the drawstring and poured out a few coins into his hand. The coins glinted a golden-green colour in the moonlight. "Please," he said, "please, please . . ."

Xeda regarded the coins stashed there on the man's palm and he found himself wondering how long it had been since he had seen money, down here, in the Threaded Pit, he supposed that money had become something abstract, something *irrelevant*.

What use did he have for money?

He couldn't *eat* money.

"Please, please," the sailor continued, his lower lip trembling now, and his cheeks, now that Xeda fully considered them in the moonlight, were almost a pale shade of blue.

Xeda thought long and hard. It had been a long time since he'd revealed himself to someone, was now the time? Was it time for him to make his reappearance to the world?

. . . Because if this man returned to his civilisation, if he escaped the Threaded Pit, there was no telling what they might do if they found Xeda to be alive here.

Would they come for him?

Come to kill him at last, just like they'd promised to do before?

. . . Or would they leave him be to live out his half-life in the shadows, feeding off rats and lichen from the rocks. Condemned to feed off whatever happened to float by.

Just like this man had floated by right now.

Decisions, decisions, decisions.

Never easy.

He toyed with another leap from the shadows, but something about the man, something about that *pitiful* look of his, it just spoke to him, touched something deep inside himself. Because, in this man, he recognised something of himself.

Or was his mind just playing tricks again, when his belly told the cold, hard truth?

He stepped out from the shadows, and parted his cloak, revealing himself to the man.

6

THE MAN'S GASP appeared to linger in his throat a while, to become caught there as if a spider had weaved its web about the roof of his mouth. There were spiders here, of course, down here in the Threaded Pit, and it was to the man's fortune that they hadn't discovered him first.

Because there was no mortal sympathy to them at all. The man never would've had another chance . . . like the one he had now.

The coins, one by one, slipped from the man's palm, and landed all about him—scattered—pinging down onto the pebbles and nestling about him in the crunched-up sand. His whole body became locked in an almighty shudder, and Xeda, just for a second, was certain the man had stopped breathing, that his body had given up on him.

But then the man spoke again.

"Who . . . Who . . ." he started, but once more could not finish.

Xeda kept his eyes sharp, fixated on the man, sitting down there, like a battered ragdoll—having been thrown about by the elements, and left like he was now. "I haf lived here."

The man's eyes widened, and he managed a reply. ". . . What?"

Xeda could no longer make the connection between his brain and his tongue. It seemed like somewhere something had become irreversibly scrambled, and that he'd never get the facility back again.

But then he thought on his master's words, what his master had always said.

Practice. Practice. Practice.

That was all he needed. He had to take it slowly. Gently. Just as he would lap the moisture from the lichen that lined the rocks. It took time, and patience.

"I am . . . *lived.*"

The sailor's shoulders stiffened, and Xeda knew that, for the first time, he was really taking in his appearance. What must he think? Xeda hadn't seen his own image for years and years now, and so he had no concept of how he might come across to others. But he knew how he lived his life, and the *things* he had to do to stay alive . . . and he could only imagine just how that had moulded his body.

"Is . . . is there . . . a . . . a . . . a . . . *way* out?" the sailor said.

Xeda cocked his head to one side, almost unable to understand the request. The way the man spoke was unfamiliar to him, those *sounds* he made almost beyond his comprehension. But he did understand. He knew what the man wished to say, and how he must respond.

Gradually, he lifted his arm up from his side, and with the crooked, bony fingers which he regarded only in the moonlight, he pointed out to sea, and said, his voice rasping the base of his throat, "Waaay ouuut."

The sailor's shuddering subsided just a fraction and he followed Xeda's curled-up fingernails, his *claws*, and looked out to the thrashing, unkempt sea. Then he turned back to regard Xeda once more, though he kept his eyes fixed to the ground, to the chewed-up and spat-out sand below them. "Isn't there . . . a . . . an-*another* way?"

Xeda, already feeling his throat dry and painful from the words he'd already uttered, gave the man a simple, doleful shake of the head.

The man seemed to understand, and he flattened himself up against the rock. His lips maneuvered between a frown and a smile, almost too quickly for Xeda to gauge, and the tears began to roll down his cheeks. "Will you . . . will you help me?"

Xeda stared long and hard at the man, at that cut on his arm, at the blood dribbling down his skin. That blood that he knew he could feast upon, that would be a rich, hearty meal after all those rats . . . after the *lichen*.

His heart beat slower now, and Xeda found himself more under control, as if just being around this man, attempting to *talk* with him had eased him out of the coma that had plagued him these numberless years in the Threaded Pit.

And he felt that faint *hum* through his blood, that scrap of mortality that hung about his veins, and which, apparently, refused to be totally silenced.

Was there anything else he could do?

7

OUTSIDE, on the beach, with the moonlight streaming down, Xeda felt the rays soak into his skin, send his blood flurrying about his body. That blood . . . the man's blood, still hummed in his nostrils, and he could feel his skin prickling up into thousands of pimples, the hairs all standing on end.

But he could resist. He was *determined* to resist.

The storm had calmed now, and only a breeze remained. The sea had ceased its thrashing, and steadied to a lull, as if taking a breath before resuming its violence. The violence which had capsized the man's ship and brought him here, to the Threaded Pit.

Together, they gathered the scraps of wood, the wood which had washed in with the tide. And they pawed through whatever they could use, discarding and hoarding as they made their decisions.

The gentle stirring of the pebbles beneath their feet and the light wash of the waves up on the beach were the only sounds that accompanied them.

Though Xeda could find scraps of memory, vague notions of how the pieces all fitted together, how they were intended to float a man—a *mortal*—away on the waves, he found he could hardly put that concept into his imagination. No longer did he have the capacity. His mind a frazzled, burned-out wreck which refused to bend to his whim.

And so, with all the pieces of wood gathered in, all stacked up on the beach, he watched on as the man pawed his way through them, as he discarded and hoarded to the profound confusion of Xeda.

But he watched on all the same.

When Xeda observed the moon sinking on the horizon, and that lightness enter the air, he felt that *fizzle* through his blood and knew that, soon, he would have to return. He would have to seek the refuge of the Threaded Pit.

Because, now, it was more than the simple prison it had once intended to be.

It *was* a refuge.

His beleaguerment became deeper and deeper as he observed the man making himself busy, apparently unaffected by his fatigue now, unaffected by his condition. The glimmering of the sunrise over the sea invigorated him, while it stripped Xeda.

And he shrugged his cloak back on, up his shoulder, to guard against the sting of the sunrays. He could only bear it for so much longer. Then he would have to retreat entirely.

8

XEDA was already standing in the shadow of the cave—in the shadow of the Threaded Pit—when he observed the man sliding his wooden construction down pebbles and to where the water washed up on the beach.

And Xeda watched as the sunrays licked at the pebbles, and as they brought warmth to the place, and set the man's hair in a kind of blond fire.

The vitality was almost enough to make him weep.

The water came up to the man's calves now, and the water ebbed about the wooden structure, and the man delved further into the water, into that turquoise-coloured abyss.

Or what Xeda somehow remembered, at the back of his mind somewhere, had been called 'turquoise.'

But how should he really know?

The man was looking about him, scouring the beach, though Xeda wasn't sure for what. And then his eyes came to rest on Xeda, and Xeda felt that ribbing icy surge power up through him, almost as if threatening to form icicles, cut through his skin and spill from his veins. The man gestured to him, a smile now on his face. Not like the smile the night before, when he'd been on his back in the cave. A full, healthy . . . *mortal* smile.

A smile that brought memories back to Xeda.

Things that he had forgotten, and would soon forget again.

As he turned his back on the man to return to the Threaded Pit, he heard him calling out to him, in words that Xeda could no longer understand.

And he only felt himself again once he sensed the icy shroud of the shadows of the Threaded Pit rolling back over his shoulders, back over his head. He breathed in the dank air, and flushed the fresh sea air from his lungs. Because he was back where he deserved to be.

Back where he had been put.

And where he would live forever more.

CLOTH. SKIN. BLOOD. BONE.

G REY SKIES dominated the landscape. Rain drizzled down. A chill pricked the breeze and brought the blood to the surface of the skin. Sheilds Guider crossed his arms over his chest, pressing his soaked tunic closer up to his skin. He could feel the weight of the wet cloth clinging to him. Making him slow. Making him clumsy. And he couldn't afford to be clumsy.

Not now.

He felt the raindrops landing on his bald scalp, the rough stubble which remained doing little to prevent the water from traversing the surface of his skin. The water trickled down the side of his face. Down his collar. No matter how wet he became, he never got used to the sensation. In fact, each time another drip dribbled down the collar of his tunic it was more unpleasant than the last.

He pressed his back up against the plaster wall of the house. He felt the shadows drifting over him. The moonlight still streaming down but a long way from being able to illuminate his surroundings.

Good, that was good.

Because off, over to his side, he could hear the murmur of voices.

In their tone, he could make out slurred speech.

That ever-present red flag which never failed to draw his attention.

Easy pickings.

As he slipped away from the wall, and felt the hard forms of the cobblestones through the thinned soles of the boots he had stolen off the last man he'd murdered, he thought back to Onderswort, and couldn't help but smile.

All those wretches, out there, like him, in the rain.

But the difference was that he was free.

He had *taken* his freedom.

It hadn't been difficult.

Not for him.

Only been a matter of patience.

Very few inmates of the prison colony of Onderswort possessed patience.

The reason he had been sent to Onderswort had nothing to do with a lack of patience. He had never had trouble waiting for something if he *truly* wished to obtain it. The simple fact of the matter was that—sooner or later—those like Sheilds would be weeded out of the Crystal City no matter what they did. He knew that his ethics did not square with those of the general population.

He was an anomaly.

A *deadly* anomaly.

Sheilds weaved closer to the mangled, drunken voices in the night-time darkness. He imagined he could hear their beating hearts. That he could feel each one of their thoughts as they slouched through their minds. Drunks *disgusted* him. Although he never felt bad about what he did—about what he *had* to do—he seemed to feel himself on more solid moral ground when they were *drunks*.

He could smell soaked horse flesh on the air.

That would be to his benefit if they had horses with them.

The last horse he had ridden to death and left out in a dried-up valley hundreds of miles from here. There'd been no choice except for him to leave the beast behind. And he had almost died himself escaping from that particular spot.

But he *had* survived.

That was what set him apart from ordinary men.

Whatever the circumstances.

Whatever his surroundings.

And if he was sure of one thing then it was this:

He *would* return to Ilsnare . . . the Crystal City . . . even if he died doing so.

He turned the corner.

Up ahead, he saw a pair of torches burning away; their fiery glow flickering across the cobblestones of the town square. Sure enough, he spied two horses hitched to the simple wooden post. Both of the horses were dozing. He could see—from the shape of their bodies—the strength in their flanks; that they were thoroughbreds.

So much the better.

He shifted his gaze away, to the staggering figures emerging from a back alley. Four of them. He silently swore to himself. He had hoped there would be two, at the most.

Four certainly made things more complicated.

At least without a weapon . . .

But he would get his work done anyhow.

Of that he was convinced.

He moved with the shadows, overhearing the drunken, singing voices of the men as they swayed about; out of control. Several times, one or the other of them staggered into one of the walls of the houses. Once or twice, one of the men fell to the ground while the others called out an ecstatic cheer as if it was the funniest thing in the world.

Sheilds kept a careful eye on the windows of the upper floors of the houses. He watched for the curtains, worried that he might see one of them twitch back at an inopportune moment.

But, in reality, it didn't matter.

There was one thing in common with a group attack, and that was noise. No matter how he approached this. No matter how *careful* he was, he knew that he would cause a ruckus.

The trick would be to get away.

And to get as much of their clothes—as much of their *money*— as he could possibly manage.

He crouched down below a small wall. He was thankful for the play of the light. He knew that if it had been day, or if the men had had their full wits about them, then his hiding place would've been ill-thought-out, at best. He listened to their footsteps, closing on the horses.

He breathed in deeply, readying himself; channelling his strength.

Just one chance to get the upper hand.

Then these men—no matter what sort of a state they were in —would strike back.

2

THE WORLD BLURRED as Sheilds leaped up from behind the wall.

Flame.

Shadow.

Moonlight.

Acting quickly, he grabbed the back of the last man's travelling cloak. He yanked it hard. He listened to the man make an elongated gagging sound. Trying to call out to his companions—pacing on ahead of him—but he couldn't find the words.

Couldn't find the *strength* to form words.

Sheilds watched on as the other three men meandered their way toward the horses.

He had to be quick.

Efficient.

This was his chance.

Sheilds gripped the man by his throat, from behind. He twisted his neck with sudden fury and heard the *snap* of his spine. He allowed the dead weight to drop down. Once on the floor—never looking away from the other three men as they approached the horses—he stripped the man of his cloak. That done, he threw the cloak over his shoulders, feeling the satisfying weight of a purse within. At least the men hadn't spent *all* their coins on drink this evening.

Even still wearing his soaking-wet tunic beneath the cloak, he felt a sudden warmth plough through his blood. Perhaps it was the knowledge that, when he got the opportunity, he would find himself a hot bowl of soup at some wayward tavern. Tonight he would need to travel, of course, and travel *quickly*. But, later. Later he could *enjoy* himself.

One of the men called out.

Sheilds struggled to understand the dialect.

Were they even speaking his language?

He had never had a talent for the tongues of others.

He had never taken much interest in the living beyond what they had to give him in death.

Another voice joined the first.

It pricked Sheilds's ears.

He glanced up briefly.

Saw the pair of grinning, drunken faces peering into the darkness.

No doubt they were expecting some more high-jinks.

Some *hilarious* happening.

That their friend had taken a tumble and was in need of a helping hand to find his feet again.

Their friend would need a little more than a helping hand ...

They continued to call out.

Sheilds held himself very still, wrapped in the cloak.

Slowly, making sure to place the hood over his head, he rose from his crouched position. He made a slight staggering motion, the best he could muster, and was greeted with a *cackle* of laughter from the remaining trio.

No, he absolutely couldn't make out their words.

They were nothing but gibberish to him.

But Sheilds kept his gait steady, so that they wouldn't expect.

And he continued to approach them.

Once he was close enough to touch the cloth of their clothing, they had already turned their backs to him, and begun the elaborate process of clambering up into the saddles of the fine beasts of theirs. When one of the men had got onto the back of his horse, he reached down a shaky hand for Sheilds, helping him up onto the saddle behind him.

Sheilds took his hand from him.

And he was surprised at the man's strength in lugging him aboard.

The man jabbered something, but, judging from the chuckles which followed, Sheilds was not expected to reply.

The man jabbed the horse with his heels and set them off across the cobblestones.

Sheilds slowed his breathing ... telling himself to be calm.

It really was as simple as that.

3

THEY PLODDED ON out across the grassy plains, leaving the village, and its torchlight, in their wake. Sheilds couldn't quite believe how these men suspected nothing . . . how they did not realise that there was something poisonous in their midst.

But he supposed it was a case of 'more fool them'.

If only they had remained sober tonight they might have had a scrap of a chance of escaping with their lives.

As Sheilds clung onto the man sat on the horse before him, he eyed a dagger hanging from his belt. He knew that he would have to take care. No matter how drunk these men were, they were sure to notice the earthy *thump* of their companion hitting the ground. And, even if they didn't hear him hit the ground, then surely they would eventually notice that only one person remained seated upon the horse. There was also the matter of the scream to consider, because a drunken man was much more likely to be set reeling with confusion at sudden pain—at sudden death—than even a sober man. As it was, Sheilds allowed the man to ride them on further, knowing that he should wait his moment. And, after what must've been ten minutes' riding, he was glad that he had done.

The two men on the horse ahead led them through a forest trail, through a group of pine trees. It was an odd sensation to see nothing but the darkness on either side, pressing up against them. The moonlight found it difficult to beam down through the branches of the trees. As they rode on through the forest, Sheilds was certain that he could feel the steady glare of animals focussing upon them . . . just as much evil upon their minds as Sheilds.

On the other side of the forest, Sheilds spotted the pair of cottages—the lights turned down low now—and an involuntary smile curled the corners of his lips.

All the lights were out in the cottages, of course.

The families all in bed.

The wives, apparently, resigned to seeing their husbands when the sun next rose up over the horizon. More fool them . . .

Seeing his destiny open out before him, Sheilds silently slipped the dagger out of its sheath. The man riding ahead didn't so much as flinch at the sensation. When he held the blade to the man's throat, it all seemed to happen so easily. It was only when he felt the slight ripple of muscle—the man preparing to let loose a scream—that he jabbed the blade in behind the windpipe and ripped forward. All at once silencing the man.

The horse's flanks quivered slightly as Sheilds tossed the man off the side of the horse.

He listened to him land in the long grasses alongside.

He turned his attention back to the other two men; on the horse ahead.

They only rode on.

Not even bothering to look back.

No doubt they only had their beds—and the warmth of their wives—on their minds now.

He was certain that the furthest matter from their thoughts was death.

Soon, though, it would be the foremost matter.

The *only* matter.

4

K NOWING NOW that he could not possibly remain in sight of the men, however drunk they were, Sheilds quietly steered his horse down the slope of the cottage. He dismounted the horse and tied its reins about a dead trunk which stuck up from the ground.

He turned his attention upward.

To the cottage.

His heart gave thick, steady beats.

He squeezed the leathery grip of the dagger, feeling the stickiness of the man's drying blood. It seemed almost to act as a second skin against the night-time chill. Although he understood nothing of the men's words, he could tell—from the smooth, slurring tone and gentle hilarity of their voices—that they had hardly been flung into a panic by what had transpired.

It appeared that their companions having gone missing on the ride back home from the tavern was something of a frequent occurrence.

Sheilds watched their silhouettes as the men went about preparing their horses to rest from the night's ride. Even though the two men were clearly afflicted by the drink they'd poured down their gullets earlier, this was the sort of knowledge that was so deeply embedded that it wouldn't ever entirely leave them . . . probably not even in sleep.

As Sheilds climbed the slope, the dagger down at his side, he continued to listen to their baffling conversation. He listened to their staggering gait, trying to judge what should be his approach.

In the end, he waited until one of the men had taken several steps down the slope, and his companion had slipped from sight for several moments.

Acting on an impulse which Sheilds was certain he shared with a cat, he lurched forward, grabbed hold of the beleaguered man and neatly slit his throat with the same blood-stained dagger with which he'd dealt with his companion.

This time, the man *did* struggle.

Even as the hot blood ran down his front, he gripped tightly to Sheilds's arm.

His fingertips jabbed into Sheilds's skin.

It almost—*almost*—gave Sheilds pause for thought.

Almost made Sheilds believe that he was going to have a fight on his hands.

. . . But just like his other two companions, the man slipped through Sheilds's fingers.

He slumped at his knees and crumpled into a pile in the long grasses.

Once Sheilds had padded the man's body—once he had uncovered the man's purse—he wondered if he should bother with the last remaining man . . . or if he should merely be contented with the work he had performed thus far.

He *had* done good work, after all.

In the end, though, Sheilds knew that he would have to take care of the fourth, and final, man or else it could mean great trouble for him. Even in his drunken state, the man was bound to realise his companion had disappeared; and was *bound* to strike out looking for him.

A drunken man could just as easily raise the entire house as a sober one.

And that meant more complications.

That an alarm would be raised.

Torches would be lit.

A chase would commence.

And although Sheilds fancied his chances in escaping the

clutches of any such search, he was equally unenthusiastic to have such a search take place.

He wanted to simply slip away into the night.

With nobody having seen his face.

So he focussed his attention on the last remaining man as he busied himself with his horse, going through the mechanical, everyday motions as familiar to him as the act of scrubbing himself down with soap suds. He felt a delightful thrill pass through his veins.

Blood pumped up to his temples.

As he had the first time he'd felt another man's blood flow down his forearms, he felt *alive*.

Like he was truly doing what the gods had designed for him.

That he was seizing what the world had to give him.

Determined *not* to let go.

Perhaps it was a twig snapping beneath the sole of his purloined boots, or maybe it was some stirring of an animal in the distant trees. Whatever it was, when Sheilds closed within about a dozen paces, the man turned around.

Stared back into the darkness.

He spoke to Sheilds.

This time, though, it was a language Sheilds understood.

Thick with an accent.

"Who is there?"

Sheilds held himself back. He didn't respond, even though the man could clearly see the form of his body in the dark. When it became clear that the man wasn't going to simply return to his work, forget that he had seen anything—*anybody*—at all, Sheilds took another few steps forward.

Unafraid to hide the dagger down at his thigh.

The man's eyes wandered for several moments.

They wandered over the blade.

Over the dried blood on the metal.

Then he turned his attention upward.

"Who are you?" he asked, meeting Sheilds's eye. "What have you done?"

Both questions lingered in the air, unanswered.

He knew by their context that the man realised just what had happened tonight.

Perhaps the man wasn't as drunk as Sheilds had made himself believe.

Maybe the man was really stone-cold sober.

At least his speech wasn't slurred.

Sheilds held himself still, his grip tightening about the dagger, ready to act if the man attempted to cry out for help—ready to save his own skin.

"It's none of your concern," Sheilds finally replied.

Even in the darkness, Sheilds observed the man blink several times, as if he didn't comprehend Sheilds's answer. As if he didn't *understand* how what Sheilds said could be so.

Perhaps he was still wrapping his mind around the fact that his companions were dead.

Although Sheilds had always been an outsider—and always would be—he understood how people became attached to the humans around them; inhabiting their otherwise empty days. There was even a term for it; one which he had heard uttered all over the kingdom:

Shock.

Was this man in *shock*?

The man continued to stare back at him with wide eyes.

His lips were parted slightly.

But he made no gesture to call out for help.

Perhaps Sheilds would be lucky.

Maybe he was *due* some luck.

Finally, the man spoke, "Please," he said, his voice husky, and, although unshaking, a strong scent of alcohol carried on his breath, "I would like to beg . . . to beg that you take me with you."

Sheilds's chest tightened.

His gut churned about.

He glanced behind, certain that the man might be attempting some delaying tactic so that—unbeknownst to Sheilds—another snuck up behind him and struck him on the head.

There was nobody in the shadows, though.

Sheilds had become extremely adept at being able to spot humans anywhere at all.

Compared to the animals who made nature their home, they caused such a fuss.

Snapped branches.

Earth cracking beneath their stride.

Their relentless groans of exertion.

But there were no humans here; none except for Sheilds and the man.

And that was when the truth struck him.

Sheilds stared at the man before him, then finally said, "Mage?"

The man held himself still for several seconds before he brought his hand up in front of their eyes. From his palm, a spark flashed in the darkness . . . and then caught.

A single flame sprung up from his skin.

It illuminated their faces.

Sheilds knew he could no longer leave the man alive now.

The man had *seen* his face.

The man could be used as part of the effort to track him down.

Something which Sheilds, quite simply, could not allow.

"I don't fit in here," the man continued, his voice lower; somewhat firmer.

The flame continued to flicker away on his palm.

Sheilds tilted his head to one side, taking in the multitude of colours—not just a fiery orange but with greens and blues and browns and *blacks* all mixed in there. Ever since Onderswort, Sheilds had found himself swept up anew in the wonder of fire. In the simple marvel of creating such warmth and light from nothing more than a simple spark and a few dead leaves.

"Please," the man went on, closing his fist, and finally extinguishing the flame. "Won't you take me with you?"

5

SUNRISE ILLUMINATED the ragged line of the horizon; bringing into view the pine trees which stood about on all sides. Dawn was commencing. He could hear the *twitter* of bird-song all around.

Birds rising with the new day, some sort of fresh optimism afflicting them; the optimism that today might be a better day than the last. He supposed he couldn't blame them.

Most creatures needed some sort of hope.

. . . Or else they might go crazy in this *Crystal* Kingdom.

He felt his horse's gentle breathing. He squeezed the beast's flanks with his thighs. He had thought long and hard about bringing another horse along with him; that with the supplies he might easily have snatched the night before he would need another horse to carry them.

But, in the end, he had been forced to leave many things behind.

If someone did come after him, then he would need to be nimble.

Able to *disappear*.

He could only afford to carry with him that which he could wear on his body.

For whatever reason, he knew that he had to keep on living; whatever the cost.

Perhaps it was because he had made it this far, to Ilsnare—the Crystal City—that he was simply determined that nothing would stand in his way.

Not even a fire mage.

As he felt himself slipping away among the rhythmic fall of his horse's hoofs, he thought back to the scene. To how he had surprised that mage by slipping his dagger up through the base of his ribcage . . . robbing him even of the chance to speak some choice last words . . . the man, the mage, had been so certain he would agree to his request; that he would *take* the mage with him.

That alone had been sufficient reason to kill the mage.

And then to turn his attentions to the pair of cottages.

To kill all those, still sleeping, within.

Although he knew little of magic, he knew enough that he understood the capacity of mages to speak into one another's minds, with no need for words. And he also knew that magic was not something which, of itself, appeared in a Mortal's veins . . . no it carried through from the father to the child . . . which meant that Sheilds had had to cover his tracks.

He couldn't afford to take chances.

Men, women, children.

They all had to die.

Lest one of them be left with the impression of Sheilds's face etched in their minds.

When they grew—*or perhaps before*—they would come after him.

With everything they had.

No, it had been better that Sheilds covered his tracks.

Because if he didn't take care of yesterday then how was he ever meant to take care of today?

Feeling the weight of the purses which clung to the inside of his travelling cloak, he nudged the horse on a little harder. He hoped to make a tavern before nightfall. With the cash he'd plundered he would live like a king. Or, at the very least, a favoured knight.

A favoured knight of the devil himself.

FEAST OF GIVING

S ANT'ARC could feel her stomach grumbling away. She carried the fattened pheasant. Felt its warm feathers brush up against her bare forearms. Could feel its enquiring head twitch from side to side as it attempted to make sense of the world with its bird brain.

Every couple of steps, it let out a tiny *pluck-pluck* cry.

The bird smelled, like all birds did, faintly of earth and excrement. And, despite herself, Sant'arc couldn't help thinking about the rich, succulent odours—not to mention *tastes*—the bird would give off once her mother set it boiling in a pot. Sometimes, at night, while she lay on her straw mattress, staring at the wooden ribs of the ceiling—the beams which marked the underside of the roof of her house—Sant'arc wondered if animals felt pain like mortals did.

Or if it was such a different prospect that it didn't even bear comparison.

And, if so, how was it different?

How did animals *see* the world at all?

Was their vision so blurred as to be useless?

Were they totally dependent on their sense of smell?

Their sense of *taste*?

Did they *feel* the approach of predator or prey through the ground, through their paws?

Or could they *hear* it coming a mile off?

Whenever Sant'arc did realise she was wondering about animals, she silently scolded herself, knowing what her father's— or her mother's; for that matter—response would be.

They would, as always, tell her to put her mind to other things.

Such as what would be her trade . . . what might she *dedicate* herself to?

And Sant'arc couldn't think of anything at all.

She was a terrible seamstress, and her cooking was just horrifying.

Whenever she thought about going further afield, offering herself—perhaps—in Ilsnare, the Crystal City, as a wash woman, or a handmaiden, she simply couldn't get herself excited. Her parents often chided her for not having settled on an occupation. Once the Feast of Giving came to an end she would be forced into her destiny.

One way or another, she would leave home.

And the only thing which Sant'arc could really ever believe herself doing was dedicating her life to the understanding of animals and their nature.

But there was little chance of that.

Scholars, as Sant'arc knew, were all male.

And, even if Sant'arc *had* been born with the 'correct' natural attributes, it would've been an uphill battle for her to find a patron. Somebody *willing* to fund her studies. No, even if she had wished it—even if she had *had* the resources—it was far too late for her to attend advanced schooling. Next year, she would pass her twentieth summer.

Why, by most measures, she would be an old maid!

She kicked at some loose stones in the yellow, dirt path. She watched them skitter off out of the way of her boots, pinging into tarpaulins of the market stalls. She breathed in deeply, feeling the scrub of the dusty air marking her throat.

Just another day in Geyt.

The town where she had been born.

And where she would *die*.

It hardly seemed worthwhile that she had bothered to put on

her very best dress—the one which her father had acquired for her last year, when she had completed nineteen summers—because now it was covered in the distinctive, yellow dust of Geyt. She thought about all she had heard of the wider world—of Shel-lacnass—about snow, and frost, and ice; and she had to use all the imagination she had to conjure *those* ideas. All she knew of the world was Geyt's blinding heat.

Day after day.

Bringing sweat lolling out from pores.

Never-ending.

Brutal.

As if the world responded to her despondence, Sant'arc realised she could smell strawberries.

Fresh. Sweet. Full of life.

She turned to look.

Observed a stall selling tea.

She eyed the large, metal pot which contained the reddish liquid.

What *wouldn't* she give to have a taste?

There was so much in this world—in all of *Shellacnass*—that she had never had a chance to encounter for herself. And, following the Feast of Giving, she would never have a chance again.

That thought set her mind reeling. On a rather *wicked* thought. Something which she could never—*ever*—do . . . but she thought it all the same:

Run away.

S ANT'ARC DRAGGED BACK the dirtied cloth which blocked the entrance to her family home.

Immediately, she felt the warmth passing through the air, she breathed in the harsh odour of cooking onions, and garlic. Her mother, already, was preparing the garnish for the pheasant which Sant'arc had brought home. Which she had been *supposed* to bring home.

With each step into the home, as the sound of her sandaled feet softened against the elaborate rugs, she could feel her heart throbbing in her ears.

Her mouth tasted dry.

And she heard bells ringing in her skull..

This could be an awful mistake . . . a *horrible* mistake . . . or it could be a new beginning altogether. She had to take the chance.

She felt herself almost rendered hypnotised by the delicious odours coming from the kitchen, and it seemed like things unfolded all too quickly. She was arriving at the moment which might decide her fate. And without fanfare.

Before she knew it, she stepped in over the threshold, and stood looking into the kitchen.

Her mother stood with her back to her, working busily, chopping vegetables and then dropping them into the pot bubbling away on the stove.

She could see that—like always—her mother was wearing her working clothes. The slightly rumpled, once-white robes. She eyed the tightened strings which held her apron on at her front, as they criss-crossed over her shoulders, squeezing a bulge of fat beneath her clothes.

"Santi?"

Sant'arc swallowed hard.

This was it. She would just come out with what had happened . . . with the *lie* she had cooked up on her way home. "Yes, mother?"

Her mother turned and eyed her. At first, she drew a smile out of her lips, and then, as her gaze moved downward, to Sant'arc's arms, any trace of her smile disappeared.

Her eyes met Sant'arc's once again.

"The pheasant?"

Sant'arc felt her chest tightening. The moment she had waited for. The lines she had rehearsed more than a dozen times in her head on the way home from the market stalls. They all seemed to desert her now . . . but, from somewhere, deep within herself, Sant'arc managed to find something.

To scoop out some sort of *coherence*.

"Mother," Sant'arc said, already feeling the tremble in her voice as she prepared the lie. "The pheasant—it *escaped*."

Her mother stayed very still for a long while. Her grey eyes didn't leave Sant'arc's, and Sant'arc was convinced that her mother saw right through her lie . . . and why *wouldn't* she?

Just who did Sant'arc think she was?

As good as telling stories as those hobblesmen who often passed through Geyt?

No, her mother had raised her.

She knew *all* her habits.

When her mother replied, she kept her voice straight, and even; and Sant'arc could hardly believe the cool and calm tone . . . though, equally, Sant'arc couldn't help wondering if it was all the precursor to a blustery storm.

A dusty wind.

"Tell me how it happened," her mother said.

Sant'arc poked her tongue hard into her bottom row of teeth.

She felt all the ridges of the enamel. That bitter, *tasteless* flavour. Sometimes, when she really worked at a sore in her mouth, she could draw blood from it. And, in some strange way, the flavour of blood roused something in her.

Sant'arc turned her attention back onto her mother. "I . . . well, it was . . . it happened so quickly." She was already aware that her tone of voice was wavering all over the place. She needed to be swift—*sharp-tongued*—if she was to stand a chance of convincing her mother. "I was walking through the market. It was just after I had got hold of the pheasant—and I was taking extra special care to keep it tucked into my stomach. I remembered all you said about them squirming away, wriggling through even the firmest of grasps if they could only catch the person unawares."

Here she really wanted to summon tears, and, to her surprise, they came readily. Perhaps it was the strong scent of onions in the air. She had always been somewhat susceptible to their powers.

Or maybe it was because of what she was doing.

Lying to her mother.

When she felt the first tear roll down her cheek, she noticed her mother's eyes trace it. Sant'arc waited until the tear hung right on the tip of her chin before she wiped it away.

Then continued.

"But then . . . *then* this little boy—I think he was one of the twin boys of the Lleightweiyhs—he dashed out from beneath one of the stalls, from under the tarpaulin. And, and . . . I don't know how it happened. He managed to get in—*beneath my feet*—and I . . . I *tripped* . . . fell head over heel."

Sant'arc paused for a long moment.

She could feel the raw intensity of her mother's gaze.

Then she finished the tale.

"The pheasant. It squirmed right out from my grasp. And . . . and it got away from me."

In those last words, she felt her voice break. She knew the gravity of what she had done. Of those unspoken—and yet *unbreakable*—rules which existed within her family.

Nothing was higher prized than honesty.

Why, she could recall, even from being a young thing, toddling about the house in the raw heat—the dust floating about the air—and having her father come home to decry some wily act of a merchant at the market, and how he would curse him right down to his soul.

Now Sant'arc had really done it.

She had ensured that she could *never* come back.

And that made her tears flow all the more.

Down her face.

It was then that her mother's resistance broke. Her grim, penetrating expression softened beyond recognition. She wiped her hands on the sides of her apron. Smiled widely. Her eyebrows dipping down in concern. "Oh, *dear*." And then she embraced Sant'arc.

As she put her arms about her mother's doughy body, stared over her shoulder, to the bubbling pot of vegetables just beyond, she couldn't help but feel a prickling sensation down deep in her gut.

The feeling was impossible to shake.

S ANT'ARC SET TO WORK beside her mother, the two of them working away silently, chopping vegetables. Popping them into the pot. There was nothing that could be done.

Sant'arc's father, that day, before he had set off for work, had left only enough money behind for the vegetables and a pheasant. Those were the very worst moments of the afternoon, knowing that her father would be coming home, expecting to have a wonderful, Feast of Giving meal awaiting him. With a nicely stewed pheasant to top it all off . . . he would get nothing but stewed vegetables.

Night had fallen, and the air had begun to cool, when Sant'arc heard the distinctive *creak-creak* of her father tying his horse to the rusted-up chain which hung from the outside wall of their house.

And—just like always—she heard him hock and spit in the dirt outside. Unlike other men in Geyt, her father made a point of *never* spitting indoors. Some days, when Sant'arc overheard conversations with her mother, chatting with other housewives about town, she would listen in to the other housewives pleading for counsel on how to make their own husbands more manageable.

Perhaps this was another thing which Sant'arc found sickening.

How these women did nothing but dedicate themselves to their husbands.

To dwell in the small victories: managing to have their husbands spit outside, or dust themselves off before stepping over the threshold, or the thousand other things which *men* seemed compelled—by some force of nature—to do.

What a *half*-life for those women!

As Sant'arc brushed the rest of the herbs she had been slicing into the pot, her mother turned to her and said, "Aren't you going to greet your father?"

Sant'arc, remembering herself, recalling that—*everyday, whenever she was at home*—she would be the one to go to her father. Take his travelling cape for him. And his hat. How she would ask him whether he would like some tea, or if he would like a little ale.

And she would bring him whatever he asked for.

She couldn't help wondering, even with all the disparate thoughts spinning through her mind that terrible evening, whether this might be the life that awaited her beyond her family home. To be the *housekeeper* of some so-called nobleman, left at home to scrub floors, and clothes, and dishes, while he jigged back and forth fighting mages, and the like.

The very idea was *intensely* depressing ...

Sant'arc, not realising that she was mimicking her mother until it was too late, wiped her hands on the sides of her dress, and headed off to greet her father. She almost forgot herself as she left the kitchen. But, right at the last, she remembered to grab a carrot off the surface and carry it with her.

Her father's horse would never forgive her for overlooking such an important item.

As she padded out over the threshold, to look at her father, working to tuck away the bridle straps and to remove the saddle, she couldn't help but notice that, beneath his arm, he held—with great care, but also extremely *firmly*—a pheasant.

She attempted to work out whether it was the same pheasant she had acquired that afternoon ... but, despite her self-professed love of animals, even she would've admitted that she had some great trouble telling pheasants apart.

They just all looked the *same*.

It was only when her father was through with removing the

saddle, laying it to rest down in the dirt for the time being, that he caught her eye.

His expression was stern.

Uncompromising.

She couldn't help but think back to those other times, those other evenings of the Feast of Giving, when her father would arrive with his horse laden down with presents for her, and a brimming, *wide* smile all across his face. The Feast of Giving was the only day of the year when her father wouldn't head out of the house just after dawn—to go to work.

Today, though, he certainly *wasn't* smiling.

She looked to the horse, to the horse which her father had never permitted her to name, but which she had secretly—at least in her own mind, and when she and the horse were together, out of earshot—called 'Tora-Haart'.

Her father had always argued that his horse was nothing more than a tool.

A means for him to get from one place to another.

And she did understand him—she understood why he was so cold.

She knew that, in the past, he had surely lost horses.

And after growing close to them.

Her father brushed past her, the pheasant beneath his arm. He didn't pause as he passed over the threshold, muttering over his shoulder, "Take care of the horse."

Sant'arc felt as if every muscle in her body drew taut.

Her heart beat in her throat.

Harder than she could ever have imagined.

Without thinking, she turned her attention to the horse—to Tora-Haart.

She about re-entering her own home. It was as if—only standing outside, alongside Tora-Haart—she could feel the throb of her father's ire passing through the exterior walls of the house. She had always witnessed her father's anger second-hand; never directed at herself, or at her mother.

Now, though, she caught the impression that it was, very much, directed at her.

After having taken more than twice as long as was really necessary to brush the dirt from Tora-Haart's coat, and from the saddle and bridle straps, she knew that she couldn't resist any longer. That she had to return inside.

She glanced up and down the road.

Ordinarily, there would be people weaving in and out of the houses—the street would be a frenzy of activity. But this was the eve of the Feast of Giving, and all were inside, having their dinner, perhaps a drink—looking forward to tomorrow.

Never had Sant'arc felt so alone.

And yet, there was nowhere else for her to go.

Except inside.

Sant'arc glanced to Tora-Haart, found herself uttering some inanity about the horse wishing her luck, and then she crossed the threshold to her fate within.

4

THE SILENCE within was overwhelming.

Sant'arc supposed that if she had returned to the house to see her father rushing from one side of the room to the other, destroying everything in his path, then she would've understood . . . it would've *frightened* her, but she would've been *easily* able to understand.

The quiet, though, was most unnerving.

She thought about heading to her bedroom, as if she was a girl of only seven summers.

But she wasn't seven summers old any longer.

She would be a woman soon.

Too soon.

She drew in a deep breath, right to the very bottoms of her lungs, and trod—taking infinite care—across the stone floor. And stood in the kitchen doorway.

Within, as if taking place in some other reality, she spied her mother and father.

Her mother stood with her back to her, stirring away at the metal pot.

The vegetables bubbling away within.

Her father, too, had his back to her.

He worked to defeather the pheasant.

She recalled how, this morning, she had secretly thought about asking her father whether he would allow her to watch him preparing the pheasant. She had something like a rampant curiosity which drove her to want to see exactly what was inside. Before it got cooked.

Now, though, that wasn't a prospect.

The father-daughter moments, she knew, were long gone.

Consigned to the past.

Forever.

Finally, when her father raised his head, slipped a glance over his shoulder, she sensed his cool, hard tone. That same tone, she was sure, he used to drive a hard bargain with fellow merchants . . . and especially when he was certain that they were *cheating* him.

Just as Sant'arc had *cheated* him.

Her father was quite simple, plain, with his interrogation. "Why did you lie to your mother?"

Sant'arc felt her shoulders lock up. She glanced to her mother, who only kept her back toward her, as if she was ashamed to so much as acknowledge that Sant'arc was there.

As if she was ashamed to admit, even with a glance, that she had given birth to her.

Sant'arc had no reply for her father—*what* was she to say?

"I . . ." she began, but her throat closed up.

Her father was patient.

He waited for her, and then, seeing that she was unable—or *unwilling*—to respond, he said, "On my way back into Geyt, I thought to stop by the market stalls." He busied himself plucking the pheasant, tugging the feathers out with well-focused strength.

Nothing about him spoke of anger.

Or disappointment.

Everything was numb.

"I got to speaking with Malya, and he informed me that he'd seen you a little earlier, in the market stalls, with a pheasant of your own beneath your arm."

Pluck. Pluck. Pluck.

Pluck.

Her father didn't let up with his efforts to prepare the pheasant. His head didn't shift away from his work. Not even for one moment.

"He told me that he witnessed you trading the pheasant with a tea merchant, with one of those who travels across the plains. That you handed the bird over in exchange for a large cup of that strawberry tea." He paused for a moment, staring down at his work. At what he had achieved so far with his pheasant. Ever so slowly, he turned to her. "Is that true?"

She blinked several times. It was her father's tone of voice. She wanted him to fly into a rage. But he had always been a calm man. This time she did manage to find her voice. "I . . . the merchant told me he would let the pheasant free—into the wilds. That it would be safe. That he would only take a few feathers in exchange for the tea. He wasn't planning to *eat* the bird."

Even as she spoke the words, she realised that it made no difference.

There was *no excuse* for what she had done.

Her father remained still, his eyes fixed on hers for long seconds, and then he nodded. "Prepare the table." He turned back to his preparations of the pheasant.

5

SANT'ARC FELT the silent tears roll down her cheeks. They felt cold compared with the warm air of Geyt. She could feel herself trembling all over. As she set the cutlery—all those fine things which her father had obtained through years of trading—she couldn't help but feel that she had done nothing to deserve this.

Any of this.

Just for having been her father's daughter, was that what allowed her such a life?

... And to have it come crashing down so suddenly.

To be cast out of the house—just as all women were when of age.

To make her own living.

And all when she hadn't even made her mind up yet!

One of the silver forks slipped from her grasp. It tumbled down. Landed with a *clatter* on the stone floor. She listened out for any sign that her parents had noticed this slip. She heard no response from the kitchen.

Where her mother prepared the vegetables.

Where her father prepared the pheasant.

She crouched down, to retrieve the fork.

Only when she straightened back up did she find herself looking out through the entrance to her home ... to *her parents'* home ...

All she had planned. She simply *had* to do it now.

Mind made up, she laid the silver fork on the table and then shifted for the entranceway.

She took her travelling cloak as she left.

It was so easy in the end.

Though she expected her mother or father to rush from the house, to come running after her, shouting out for her to return, neither of them came.

She was quiet.

She had prepared well.

She had left Tora-Haart all ready for riding.

Saddle freshly swept.

A carrot in her belly.

She had stowed provisions in the saddlebags.

As she rode away from her parents' home for the final time, feeling the cooling evening breeze stroke her cheeks, she thought about her plans. About how she had bet on her father stopping by at the market stalls. About how there would be one merchant who would be simply unable to keep his mouth shut . . . but she had expected her father to fly into a rage, to give her a *reason* to blaze out of the house. In the end, though, it had been something of an anti-climax.

Her father had been cold.

But shown no anger.

She had had to take the initiative herself.

It was only as she drove Tora-Haart—her hooves slipping and sliding from fatigue—on along the dirt path which wound up and away from Geyt, that she thought to stop before she turned the corner to the other side of the hill. One final look back at her parents' home.

All she had known:

Her *village.*

Geyt.

And as she stared hard at her parents' home, she couldn't help but think about how they would be there forever. Ready and waiting for her to return.

They would stay here.
And she would be back.
One day.

THE EYE

D ENZULLA ARBERBROOK listened to the whisper of the draught blowing in beneath the shabby wooden door. She felt the chill bring goose pimples dancing over the surface of her skin. She drew her traveller's cloak a little tighter up to her throat. But it did nothing to ward off the trembling which afflicted her body. She again peered through the hole in the door, to the street outside.

She could just make out the surface of the River Ils, and, she thought, the sickly sweet odours of sewage carrying on the air. As the odour had done ever since she'd been a little girl, it seized her mouth with a retch. But she tried not to let it bother her. She always felt a touch queasy this early in the morning. . . . Early morning.

These assignments almost always began in the *early* morning. That was when the Powers That Be within Ilsnare—the Crystal City—wished for surveillance to commence.

Right now, though, she saw nothing.

Nothing and no one.

When she woke with first light, when she snuck out of the tight, tiny apartment which she shared with her mother, she often swore beneath her breath at the nature of these assignments. Her mother had confronted her—more than once—claiming that she was working some kind of a second life as a prostitute . . . as if her mother had any right at all to bring into question what she did to bring food to their table. However, since the nature of Denzulla's work was top secret, she hadn't bothered to correct her mother. In fact, her mother believing that she was a prostitute was a neat cover story. And one which should also account for the type of money she brought home. The money which just as quickly filled her mother's belly. She had only ever heard her mother complain about where the food came from *after* she'd eaten her fill . . .

A fresh, biting chill drifted in beneath the door.

Denzulla chomped her teeth into her tongue. She gently reached down to the dagger which was sheathed at her belt; concealed by her cloak. As always, it sent a warmth thrill through her blood simply to reach out and set her fingertips on the handle. To know that she possessed a weapon which could *kill*. And—what was more—that there was an organisation above her which would see to her absolution if she chose violence as a course of action.

The Eye, as it was often said throughout Ilsnare, was *all-seeing*.

And while Denzulla didn't quite fall in for that melodrama—she knew that the Eye merely consisted of ordinary citizens such as herself—it was difficult to not feel as if the Eye itself embodied something much larger; something *unstoppable*. Then again, she did suppose that the Eye only stopped at the King of Shellacnass. At the feet of Louson Dorf:

The Hitchking.

Outside, she heard a scuffling.

She pressed her eye to the hole in the door again.

And could hardly believe what it was she saw.

Short, stubby figures.

All of them wearing travellers' cloaks.

Their hoods pulled up.

Dwarfs.

But, if their goal had been to pass as if nothing at all, then they had failed miserably. In fact, she believed that, if someone was right now drawing back the curtains of their bedroom window, peering down into the street, they would be alarmed to see the tiny figures toddling through the sleeping streets. Remembering her brief, that she was to 'follow and observe', she opened the door and shifted out into the street.

If she hadn't felt the full extent of the early-morning chill from within the abandoned set of rooms she'd been inhabiting previously, she certainly felt it now.

It seized hold of her entire body.

Shackled it with ice.

Froze her down to the bone.

The only thought on her mind now was of returning to her home, to her bed, to pulling the thick, woollen blankets up over her head.

But she had a job to do.

As she put one foot in front of the other, she felt the iciness clinging to the air.

A couple of snowflakes brushed against her cheek.

At the same time as she battled her trembling, she forced herself into the side of the road, into what passed for subtlety now the sun had come up.

She caught sight of the last of the dwarfs, disappearing around the end of the street.

She quickened her pace, glad that the firm, well-defined tread of her boots kept her safe from the slippery surface of the iced cobblestones. There would be nothing worse than taking a tumble at this time of day . . . of being forced to drag herself back to her feet in the wretched cold weather . . . to continue her pursuit of these dwarfs when all she really wanted—all she *really* wanted— was to return home and have her mother bubble her up some cocoa.

Once she turned the corner, she found herself facing off with a whole array of scimitars. All of them glinting gently in the early-morning light. Their blades all sharp. And each and every one of them pointed directly at the soft flesh of her throat.

She reached for her dagger.

"Move your hand again and you die—*Mortal.*"

2

DARKNESS BLED into Denzulla's vision.
It crept up on her from all sides.

And it sent a chill tingling down her spine just as willingly as the cold itself had done.

She breathed in the heady odour of earth—a smell which, on any other occasion, might've seemed somewhat homey; which might've come across as somehow comforting.

Funny how a situation could so swiftly be blurred, be switched all around, when a scimitar was held to her spine, ready to be thrust through the soft, thin surface of her skin at will.

She trudged on, deeper into the black.

Her hands had been bound with rope and they had taken her dagger off her, of course.

Like all efficient subversives, their first concern had been to neutralise the threat. They had padded her entire cloak down, taking not just her dagger but also the belt which'd held up her— several-sizes too large, third- or fourth-hand—men's trousers.

What they believed she'd be capable of doing with her belt, she really had no clue.

Then again, she was also certain that these dwarfs were merely acting with the benefit of experience. Everything they did was done with a particular reason in mind.

The dwarfs led her on for what felt like an hour, perhaps it was more, but when the dwarf in front of her came to a sudden halt, she was somewhat surprised. She had almost come to believe that they would merely keep on making her walk until such a time that she collapsed from exhaustion.

That *that* was their masterplan.

No marks on her neck from blades, or from ropes, only her

decrepit body lying in the dirt . . . a worn-out shell which had just been unable to keep putting one foot in front of the other any longer. She had heard stories—they'd often been told to her as a child—of the children who had found their way into the subterranean passageways which were known to run beneath the cobbled streets of Ilsnare like vapid veins and arteries. She wasn't certain how many of those mothers and fathers had actually ever had the chance of becoming acquainted with the passageways first-hand, or if they truly appreciated the danger inherent in them. Most likely, they only wanted to give their children a scare. So that they'd stay close—and thus *safe*—from the more tangible dangers.

The dwarfs led her through the door, and into a candlelit dug-out room.

Before she could truly absorb her surroundings, she felt the grasp of the dwarfs on either side, hauling her down onto the earthy step below. As she sat, she felt the moisture of the earth passing up through the fabric of her trousers.

The dwarfs all stood around, waiting.

One of them shut the door.

She could still sense the chilling steel of the scimitars close to her skin.

She could *feel* the sharpness of the blades.

It would take them only a moment to end her life . . . so why wasn't she afraid?

Why wasn't she scared to leave this world at a moment of their choosing?

Was it because there was nothing here for her?

Was it because of her miserable life; the life which she spent with her mother?

No, surely it wasn't that bad.

She had the money, after all.

Ever since she had begun working with the Eye, she had been able to start saving . . . saving for *what* exactly, she couldn't quite say. Perhaps she cherished secret dreams of leaving Ilsnare behind, of leaving her mother in the care of her savings while she strove out on some fresh adventure.

One of the dwarfs stood before her. He had swept back his traveller's cloak to reveal and elaborately woven woollen shirt beneath. She saw the scimitar sheathed at his waist. The weapon itself was cut down so that it wouldn't be too unwieldy for him to utilise. That meant the blade was shorter—*snubber*. She supposed dwarfs made a habit of short, sharp jabbing attacks when it came time to fight.

The dwarf had a wiry, red beard, and knitted eyebrows. His features were almost lost beneath all that hair. "What were you doing—*following* us?"

Denzulla stared back into the dwarf's black eyes, unable to quite find the words at first. Finally, though, she did. "I was headed to the markets, on the Crystal Causeway."

She surprised even herself with her cool, collected delivery.

Back when she'd first started to serve the Eye, she had come up with this as the story she would deliver were she to be captured.

She supposed—after all this time—she had begun to believe it herself.

The dwarf narrowed his eyes. "Bit early, don't you think?"

Denzulla felt the cut of a scimitar blade at the back of her neck.

Just one, well-aimed swipe.

That was all it would take.

Her life would be snuffed out as easily as the candles which surrounded them.

When she spoke again, her voice was slightly stifled. She supposed that the joint sensation of being interrogated while having a lethal weapon in close proximity wasn't entirely conducive to free thought. ". . . I wanted . . . I wanted to get there *early*."

" 'Early' ?" the dwarf said, with a slight chuckle.

She heard the other dwarfs chuckle too, almost an echo. She sensed a slight nervousness there. Why should they be nervous when they clearly had the upper-hand?

The dwarf continued in the jovial tone of his chuckle. "*I'd* say you were early," he said. "Probably several *hours* early."

"I came from out of town—I don't know how things work here . . . I didn't want . . . didn't want to get caught up in the crowds."

Denzulla was improvising now. She had never got far enough along in her imagined capture—in her imagined *interrogation*—to the point where she believed she'd need to further embellish her story. She supposed she had been naïve. She should've spent more time in her preparation. The sizeable wages she received for her service to the Eye was surely a partial means of ensuring that she would be professional in *all* aspects of her career.

The dwarf cocked his head to one side, pouted slightly. Then he glanced at another of the dwarfs, behind Denzulla. "Very well."

And she felt the blade of the scimitar dig into her throat.

3

DENZULLA'S BREATHS came panicked.
Insufficient.

Her mind slowly stitched her surroundings back together.

A faintly flickering candle gave her something to centre her attention on.

She took in the earthy walls.

On all sides.

Pit-black, now; none of those rich browns.

The famous, fertile soil produced on the plains surrounding the River Ils.

Or, at least, if the soil was thick, rich—*fertile*—then Denzulla no longer saw those qualities.

On instinct, Denzulla reached up to her throat.

She felt the scabbed-over skin.

Where the scimitar had jabbed her.

Drawn a single bead of blood.

Impossibly hot.

Impossibly painful.

And then . . . then she had passed out . . . the world had escaped her.

Slipped right through her fingers.

She snapped back to her surroundings now, to the world about her.

She was wearing the same clothes she'd been wearing that morning, when she'd left the house. They were different, now, though. Even in the dim light of this gaol cell she, apparently, found herself in, she could see that clods of mud clung to the material.

To her skin.

Entrenching the lines of her palms.

Outside, she heard voices.

The dwarfs.

Feeling her head throbbing, she sat herself upright.

Pressed her shoulders against the dirt wall.

She reached up and placed her fingertips at her temples.

Applied some pressure.

Felt the gentle jab of her pulse.

Had they done anything to her?

Slipped her some potion?

Again, she felt at her throat.

Only the smallest of nicks there from the scimitar blade. It made her gut clench to think how easily she'd been frightened into fainting . . . who did she think she was, the Princess of Shellacnass? Syre Dorf . . .

Another few moments passed, more muttering outside her gaol, and then she observed the sturdy wooden door open in on her. It was the dwarf from before. The one who had spoken to her. His red hair seemed almost black in the lack of light. He mumbled something in a language which she didn't understand and then turned to her.

"We have decided that you must be dealt with," he said.

Her throat constricted, but she managed to get out the words. " 'Dealt with' how?"

"Killed," the dwarf replied, matter-of-factly.

Her whole body went rigid.

She felt her muscles knot and her heart leap up to her throat. It took a couple of moments to regain her composure; to even be able to *attempt* to put up some sort of a carefree façade. And then she began to think rationally. She looked to the dwarf, and said, "If you wanted me dead then you would've done it already." She reached up and traced the scabbed skin at her throat. "You would have done it when you first brought me in."

The dwarf smirked, the lines of his face creasing about his mouth, but his steady, beady eyes remaining untouched. "I didn't say *when*. There is certain useful information you can give us— information about the Eye."

A tingle passed through her gut. She unfolded herself, managed to get onto her knees, and then—a touch shakily—to find her feet. She was glad to see, when she stood up straight, having to bend her neck so as not to bump her head on the ceiling, that her posture had an effect on the dwarf. That he was *visibly* cowering beneath her . . . no matter how hard he tried to hide it with that calm expression of his. She supposed that he didn't feel quite as confident when he didn't have a legion of companions, armed with scimitars, surrounding her.

That was strength.

Something worth clinging onto.

She stared back into his beady-eyed glare. "What's the Eye?" she said, doing her best to make her voice as ditsy as possible.

The dwarf attempted to keep his expression fixed. He crossed his arms and tilted his head slightly to one side. "Don't play games with us. We know far more than you could ever imagine."

"Oh, really? Then why do you need *me* to know more about the Eye?"

Even beneath the scrub of the dwarf's beard, she saw that his complexion coloured. That he was embarrassed at the direction of this exchange.

She was making him look a fool.

The dwarf unfolded his arms. Stared back at her for several moments, and then turned to leave. As he ventured on out through the door, before it slammed shut behind him, she heard him say, "We'll see who knows the most in the end."

Even though the closing door snuffed out the candle in her gaol, she couldn't stop the smile sneaking onto her lips.

A smile which warmed her from the inside.

4

I T MIGHT'VE BEEN HOURS—it might've been *days*—before
the door to Denzulla's gaol opened wide again. And when it
did, she was glad to see the clay bowl of soup which was steaming
away in the hands of the dwarf standing there.

It wasn't the dwarf from before, the one with the scrubby red
beard—the one who seemed to be in charge. This dwarf had
blond, plaited hair, and, after a brief few moments, she decided—
from the lighter gait, from the floating material worn—that this
was a *female* dwarf.

The female dwarf held out the clay bowl.

Denzulla took it from her, immediately supping at the rim.

Even though the soup was searing hot, even though she could
feel it burning her tongue, the roof of her mouth, she continued to
slurp it down. If there'd been the possibility of having a spoon,
Denzulla wouldn't have been prepared to wait. When she had
finished the bowl of soup, she handed it back to the dwarf, who
took it from her with a slight smile.

"More?" the female dwarf asked.

Denzulla wiped her lips with the back of her earth-sodden
sleeve, flashed a smile. "*Please.*"

The female dwarf returned moments later with a fresh bowl.

And Denzulla performed the same efficient disappearing trick.

That done, the female dwarf dawdled. She held the emptied
bowl down at her waist, as if distracted by what she should do
next. Finally, she asked, "Is it true?"

"Is what true?" Denzulla replied, stretching her legs out, and
preparing to lie down with a pleasantly warm knot in her
stomach.

"About the Eye?"

Denzulla breathed in deeply.

So this was the plan.

They had tried to sweat her—to leave her here in this cell for a long while—and now they had sent in this unsuspecting female dwarf with the brief of trying to draw the truth out.

Well, if that was their plan then they'd need to try a little harder.

Just as Denzulla was about to reply, in a slightly bitter tone, she held herself back.

She decided that she should play a game of her own.

"Yes," she replied.

The female dwarf flinched. "It *is* true?"

"Uh-huh," Denzulla said, turning her gaze upward, to the ceiling of the gaol. "What do you want to know about it?"

Denzulla listened intently for the sound of trudging feet nearby. She expected that the dwarfs had some means of silent communication, or, at the very least, some means of giving one another a signal that something important was happening.

That red-haired dwarf would be arriving shortly.

Of that Denzulla was certain.

The female dwarf finally regained her composure. She picked at some imperceptible mark on the rim of the clay bowl as she spoke—as if she was *embarrassed* to be saying what she was. "The Kingdom of Shellacnass. They have wanted to purge Creatures from their borders for such a long time . . . all we seek is peace."

Denzulla, of course, knew all about the political meanderings of the previous King of Shellacnass, and, especially, the former Captain of the Royal Guards, Herimyre. She wasn't sure where she stood on Creatures . . . she only did the job she was paid to do. And that, more often than not, seemed to involve observing Creatures illegally residing in Ilsnare. Like these dwarfs.

The female dwarf met Denzulla's eye. "Why do you wish to eliminate us? Can we not live among you as friends—as allies?"

Denzulla felt her heart clench.

What did this dwarf expect *her* to do?

She had hardly any clout within the Eye, let alone in Ilsnare at large.

And it wasn't like she had any information even to help them with.

The Eye was constructed in such a way so that no one member would ever know more than they needed to. Surely these dwarfs understood that?

"I don't want to eliminate *anyone*," Denzulla replied.

Apparently satisfied with this explanation, the female dwarf nodded and then retreated from the gaol, headed back out into the corridor with the clay bowl dangling down at her thigh. It was only when Denzulla heard her footsteps disappear off into the distance that she allowed herself to exhale; to finally *breathe* again.

5

ON THE DAY of her execution, Denzulla could barely keep her thoughts straight.

And it was little wonder.

She had been trapped within this tiny dug-out hole in the earth for what seemed like months now. Nobody had come looking for her. She knew that these subterranean passageways were beyond the remit—if not the *knowledge*—of the Royal Guards.

She was all alone.

Left to face her destiny *alone*.

When she heard the dwarfs approaching—saw the dwarf with the red, scrubby beard leading them—she knew that the end had come; that her time had run out.

He said nothing as he met her eye, only giving her a doleful, understanding nod.

The scimitars were out once again, and she observed how the candlelight sheened off their sharpened edges. She wondered which of these dwarfs would be the one to finish with her—to *execute* her before all the others.

Did it really matter?

Hunched over, Denzulla made her way out through the tunnels and back to the central chamber where she had been brought on her first day. There were many more dwarfs now, all of them gathered around. None of them wore gleeful expressions, although Denzulla wouldn't have expected them to. How could anyone take joy in the deaths of others?

Even if they were of a different race . . .

Finally, she was brought to her knees before the dwarfs.

She felt the red-bearded dwarf sidle up alongside her.

He whispered, gruffly, in her ear. "I hate this. I hate *all* of this . . . but we are Creatures at war, and, thus, we must act as such. Perhaps if we had been convinced of you changing loyalties we might be able to come to some arrangement . . . to some kind of agreement . . . unfortunately, though, we cannot, in good faith, allow you to go free. You know too much of our ways . . . of our *home*."

Denzulla wondered if she nodded in reply.

It felt as if she did, though she might just as easily have remained still.

The arms of the dwarfs eased her down, onto her knees, and then brought her neck out.

In the end, she rested her forehead on the cool earth.

It was a pleasant sensation.

One which—over the previous weeks—she had found to be an almost calming therapy.

Her heart beat low and even.

But for how long?

As she listened to the red-bearded dwarf address the others— his fellow Creatures—she tuned her mind out, to another place. She thought about her role in the Eye, and all the wages she'd collected.

That had been blood money, though she had never thought of it in those terms.

Now, though, she was being given a stark reminder.

The last of her life.

Her final recollection was of the distant sound of displaced air.

A *swish* of a swiftly swung blade.

Severe, sudden pain.

And then nothing.

VILLAGE OF ASHES

QUAGSMILE LAY IN RUINS.

In smoking, smouldering embers.

Looming, grisly grey clouds hovered above.

A gentle drizzle began to fall as if to complete the mockery.

Where had the rain been hours ago?

Hours ago when the fire had come ... *before* the fire had come, so that the fire might not have spread so wildly, and so fast?

Mantha reached down and fished about among the broken-up timber of what had once been her—*and her family's*—home. She was still wearing her nightdress.

There had been no time.

When she had heard the dull clanging of the fire bell, she had believed that she was still dreaming. Sometimes she had vivid, hard-to-understand dreams. Almost as real as day.

Or night.

But this had been no dream.

From within the splinters of saw wood, she located a scrap of gold wood. It was only a tiny chunk and so it had survived the fire, more or less intact. One little piece which would bring her, and her husband Hurnarth, luck in their marriage.

Even in the dim, overcast morning light, she could still see the sparkle move along the grain. She could still recall the excitement which had accompanied Tutiop—Hurnarth's brother—presenting the gold wood to them for their marriage. When work had started on their home, the next day, when Hurnarth had received Mantha's dowry, the entirety of the construction had been designed around the sliver of gold wood. The builders had been *ecstatic* to be provided with such a centrepiece. Mantha had been ecstatic, too. The only time in her life when she had felt unique.

As if she mattered more than beyond her immediate family: her husband, and her five children.

Sometimes she doubted her role in this world.

Sometimes she longed to have had the same youthful adventures as Tutiop—to have been a skuller like he was. To have met with danger head on, and to have wrestled with the cursed animals which dominated the plains of Shellacnass at night.

But those choices had never been available to her.

Not really.

Perhaps if she had been born with a penis.

Maybe if she had been born into a different family.

... If only she hadn't been expected to find a partner as soon as possible, so that she would no longer be such a burden to her mother and father.

The one girl in the family.

Like a milkless cow, or a meat-free pig, she was worthless.

She had felt secure in this world, though, for many years. For the births of all her and Hurnarth's children. Until the fire had come last night. The fire had finished with everything; the entire village. And, no matter what, no matter if they rebuilt the entire settlement from scratch, it would never quite be the same. Everyone in the village would *know* they were only a single act of nature away from having their entire world come tumbling down all over again.

Mantha rose up from her crouched position, clasping the gold wood so tightly that she felt the sharp sting of its fine splinters slipping into her skin. She brushed her nightdress, more out of habit than from a desire to do anything useful for her appearance.

She was covered in ash.

As she stroked it away from the coarse fabric of her nightdress, it clouded before her. Entered through her airways. Made her want to cough her lungs out.

She turned her head and surveyed the wreckage of Quagsmile.

People, just like her—*neighbours*—all of them grieving for their lost homes.

Their lost ways of living.

Among them she spotted Dorunarty, the finest seamstress of the Northern Villages, and the one who had threaded together Mantha's wedding dress. She was an old woman, now, of course, and her eyesight was fading. But she still possessed her uncanny ability—*a knack*—for creating the most beautiful, most imaginative, designs.

Further along, Mantha saw Fliggabard. Although only just past his fortieth summer, his hair had already turned silver. The muscles, too, which'd once marked him out as one of the finest properties of the Royal Guards of Ilsnare—the Crystal City—had withered and wrinkled in the sun, like overcooked, ruby-red great berries.

Fliggabard was approaching her, with a whole stack of charred wood in his arms. He had a determined look on his face, and as he passed her by, he politely inclined his head by way of greeting, but said nothing else.

Even now—even *so many* years later—Mantha felt her heart bounce in her chest. She remembered how during her first year of marriage, when she had arrived to Quagsmile, she had been quite taken with Fliggabard. They had first met when he had been on furlough from the Royal Guards, and she had seen him in his wispy grey uniform, with that sharp spear of his, and the crossbow slung over his shoulders. The tight, bone-crushing muscles. The well-polished, knee-high, brown leather boots.

Although she had seen skullers throughout her life, those night wardens dressed in black who kept the Northern Villages safe from harm—like her husband's brother—they had never taken her in such a way as seeing a fine man, in the summer years of his life, dressed in the uniform of the Royal Guards. She could still recall the feeling of treading her way across the cobblestoned streets of Quagsmile, her wicker basket filled with fruit and vegetables for the dinner that evening.

Fliggabard had struck her so dumbfounded that she had walked right past the road leading to her home without even noticing.

She turned to watch Fliggabard go now, and she thought of the day when he had returned to Quagsmile on a stretcher—a bandage wrapped tightly about his head, and damp with blood.

She couldn't quite ever remember being so taken aback by such a sight as that . . . and it wasn't like she had ever said anything other than, "Good morning," or other such greetings and niceties with the man. Only when she had watched him throughout his recovery, watched on as he struggled to regain his most basic of agility, that she realised that her fantasy had evaporated.

That the strapping man from the Royal Guards was gone.

Replaced by this decrepit war veteran.

Living with his widowed mother, and good only for lifting hefty items . . . like those remains of a house he carried now.

As she stood still, feeling her heart tickling her throat, she felt her husband, Hurnarth stand at her side. She felt his warming breath on the back of her neck. She could still smell the onion from the dinner she had prepared the night before. Garlic too. It seemed almost as if this was all happening in a dream, and that soon—*now*?—she would simply wake up.

She didn't wake up.

"There's a group approaching—'cross the plains."

Mantha remained lost in a daze for several moments before she snapped back to the present. She glanced about. Looked to the village walls—still very much intact; perhaps the only part of the village which'd survived the firestorm. Beyond the cobblestone walls, she could, indeed, see the shadowy silhouettes of the figures approaching.

What could this mean?

Might it be aid from Ilsnare—from the Crystal City?

No matter how much she wished to believe it might be so, the pragmatic part of her kept on nudging, telling her that it would be foolish to think such a thing. Why, the news of the fire, if it was ever carried to Ilsnare at all, wouldn't reach the city until at least nightfall.

Only when she looked to her husband again, saw the fear in his eyes, did she realise just what he was implying. But, like always, as when he was frightened, he only became calmer. His instructions were precise.

She was to take their children, dozing over on a grassy bank near the smouldering remains of their home, and to go to the stables.

Once there, they were to await instructions.

Hurnarth would meet them soon.

It took a couple of moments before the words sunk into Mantha's consciousness.

She snapped to, turned to her children, and beckoned them toward her.

2

"MA? Where we goin'?"

Mantha gripped tight to her daughter—her youngest child's—hand.

Ay'mar.

Five summers old, Ay'mar had neatly trimmed red hair, held in a messy bun around the back of her head. As if some kind of miniature imitation of Mantha, she too wore a nightdress; as did Mantha's other two daughters.

Her pair of sons, like their father, wore nothing but a pair of workman's trousers; a harsh fabric made for working the fields. The trousers which they wore had been handed down to them by their father, as Mantha, one day, would hand her own clothing to her daughters.

"To the stables," Mantha finally replied to Ay'mar, smiling as she did so, pulling off the old confidence trick which her own parents —*consciously or not*—had taught her in her own childhood; an easy way to stop the children from worrying. To take all the tension out of her voice; to make the tone flat, neutral, almost a touch *bright*.

... Because if the parent was in control, then what did the children have to worry about?

She felt the rhythmic trudge of her other children as they followed on her heels. Like everyone else in Quagsmile, they had been up half the night—the fire keeping them from sleep. Pushing them to the periphery of the village walls ... the cursed animals which loomed on the other side of the walls, on the plains, preventing them from striding out.

Mantha smelled the horses before she turned the corner. When she did turn the corner, she realised that they hadn't been the only family to have the idea of heading to the stables. As Mantha looked the place over, she immediately saw that there weren't any horses to be had.

Covered in blankets, a trio of mounds stood at the centre of the circle of people gathering.

She breathed in that stink of horseflesh again, feeling it grab her gut.

There had been other horses, of course, but she supposed they had been luckier; that they had somehow—by human hand, or otherwise—managed to get free of their tether.

To escape out onto the plains.

She wondered if they had been attacked by the cursed animals . . . if they hadn't, then they had perhaps made it to one of the many forests which surrounded the plains, and they were grazing happily; allowed to live out the rest of their lives in a sort of equine pastoral paradise, until the time they were recaptured. Sometimes, she couldn't help but envy beasts. In many ways, they seemed to have far simpler lives than she did. But, most certain of all, they were *free*.

She snapped her attention back onto the gathering crowd, seeing yet more people pouring around the corner, to the stables. More women—more *mothers*, with their own children. She recognised all their faces, automatically, without so much as a second's thought, and yet they seemed so distant from her now; almost like strangers.

Mantha reached out about herself, for each of her five children in turn, drawing them closer to her skirts lest they attempt to wander away.

Attempt to leave her sight.

Finally, sure that none of her children would get curious and leave her immediate protection, she turned to the woman—Kiona;

mother of three—and asked if she knew what he men of the village had in mind.

Kiona, with her white-blond hair and icy-blue eyes, told Mantha that the men were going to do their 'duty'. That they were going to grab whatever they could—whatever weapons they might be able to salvage—and fight off the scavengers.

It was then that Mantha felt her heart skip.

Unintentionally, Mantha found herself gripping Ay'mar's hand too tight, digging in her fingernails, and Ay'mar let out a slight *yelp*. She bent down and muttered, "Sorry, darling," to Ay'mar, in the hope of quenching her tears.

It was strange how, in times of great danger, of great *tragedy*, even children seemed to understand the gravity of the situation. At least on some level. Which was to say that they understood it *enough* to realise that there were greater matters at stake than their own personal comfort or wellbeing.

"Where's *pa*?" Mantha's eldest son, Parnraig asked.

Mantha looked him in the eye, smiled as sweetly as she dared. "He'll be along in a minute, I should suspect."

This didn't entirely convince Parnraig, who turned his head and glanced back behind them. If it came down to it, if he tried to go and be with the men—to fight off those who were closing on Quagsmile—then there would be little Mantha could do to stop him.

Parnraig, at fourteen summers old, was almost a man himself; and he would only be doing his 'duty', as Kiona had put it.

Mantha breathed heady, deep breaths.

Taking them right down to the pit of her lungs.

Although she told herself not to look, she couldn't help but return her stare to the pair of mounds covered by blankets before her; the horses which'd died in the fire the night before.

In the dawning light, she recalled how she had wondered to

herself if she had—*somehow*—cheated death. If she and her family had *meant* to perish in the fire.

She thought of how her husband Hurnarth would often shush her when she came up with such ramblings as they lay together in the blankets on the floor of their home. He would tell her that it was better for her not to mess with the gods . . . or, to put it more succinctly, for her not to *think* about them at all, lest she offend them in some way with her womanly worries and curse the season's crop.

. . . If there was no reaping to be done, then the whole family would starve.

And, not wanting to be responsible for that, she did as her husband asked.

Except for this morning.

When she hadn't been able to believe she, and her family, had survived.

Because what other explanation could there be for their survival, except for the gods' intervention?

Did it mean that she, and her family, had some other purpose?

Something that they were all supposed to do in this world?

In the Kingdom of Shellacnass?

From the other side of the cobblestone wall, Mantha heard a loud cry.

A *man's* cry.

. . . But only *one* man.

She waited for another cry to join it.

But it never came.

Her heart bounced against her ribs.

And then, feeling the eyes of everyone—all the mothers and their children—gathered there, she gently slipped her fingers free of Ay'mar's hold, and trudged back the way they'd come.

3

AS MANTHA took in the remnants of Quagsmile, reduced to ashes—*smouldering embers*—she couldn't help but feel the shock draw her muscles taut once again. It was hard to believe this ... hard to believe her eyes ... and yet, here it was.

Her focus narrowed as she felt the cool morning breeze, carrying a little warm ash which flaked against her cheeks. She turned her focus onto the round, blond man . . . dressed in pit-black, skullers clothing. He was bundling about, through the village, the men of Quagsmile standing back from him as if from shock than anything else.

Mantha saw that the man, like all skullers, wore a sword down at his side, and a crossbow strapped across his back. His cheeks were flushed, and his blond hair stood up in tufts. The image of him was such that Mantha knew he carried no threat.

That he hadn't come here, to what remained of Quagsmile, to do any sort of damage.

He was just as torn apart by the sight as they all were.

The blond skuller bundled on past Mantha, and around the corner, to the stables. It was only here that Mantha was aware of some of the village men jogging to catch up; almost as if they felt they might've made some mistake. As she turned her attention to the blond man, she saw him jabbering away at the women, begging for them to answer the question on his lips.

All the women, though, without exception, shook their heads at him.

They had no idea what or who he wanted.

Finally, the blond skuller reached Mantha.

When she breathed in, she caught the thick scent of ash and

smoke in her nostrils. She thought it strange considering the skuller had only just then arrived to the village . . . and for it to seem so potent.

"Please," he said, panting hard, sweat clinging to his face. "Can you . . . can you tell me . . . ?"

"Easy," Mantha said, forcing a smile, more to put the man, and her children, at ease than anything else. "Take it slow—we'll see if we can help you."

The skuller nodded rapidly and then drew breath. This time when he spoke, his voice—although still rushed—was clearer. At least sufficiently clear for Mantha to make out. "Toobinkra, Whollarhands," he said.

Mantha felt her whole body go rigid.

She knew the names, of course.

She knew *everyone* in the village.

The skuller was quick. He was obviously attuned to detecting people's reactions—attuned to *predicting* how people might react —as were all skullers. They needed to decide, at the snap of finger and thumb, whether or not to allow strangers through the village gates.

"They're . . . they're . . . *dead*"—he gulped at air, apparently unable to calm himself, then he met Mantha's eye with a new sharpness. "*Aren't* they?"

Mantha felt something on her shoulder, and it was only when she turned to look that she realised the skuller was gripping her tightly. His fingers were pinching her; digging *into* her skin.

Next time, the skuller shouted.

His breath was rotten.

It stank of fish and smoke.

"*Aren't they*?!"

Mantha felt the entirety of her body shake, right down to her bones. She felt herself struck dumb. She made out the women and children's faces behind the man, all of them watching her; seeing what this lunatic might do. All of a sudden, she became very aware of the sword down at the man's side, and the crossbow strapped to his back. It really wouldn't take much effort at all for him to slip it off over his shoulder and to shoot her with it at point-blank range.

She waited for someone to come to her aid, but it seemed that nobody wanted to step forward. And so she reached up, grabbed hold of the man's wrist, squeezed it tightly, and said, "Let me go."

The skuller continued to hold her. "What *happened* to them—did they or did they *not* die in the fire?"

Mantha's brain again flurried.

Of all the images which crossed her mind's eye, she wasn't certain what was real, and what was imagined. She saw the smouldering wreckage of the village which'd become her home, and she saw the twisted, charred bodies of those who hadn't been able to escape in time, and then . . . and then . . . *yes*, she saw . . . she *saw* their faces.

Determined, her mind made up, she angled her gaze upward once more.

Met with the man's eyes.

She heard the gruff, scraping tones of the men now, apparently having caught up to the invader.

She thought she heard Hurnarth's voice among them, demanding that the skuller let her go.

And yet she no longer felt fear.

She stared back into the man's eyes, confirmed what he wanted to know with nothing more than a simple nod.

The man's grip tightened suddenly, and then dropped away completely.

He seemed almost to retreat into himself.
And then he dropped down into a crouch.
Staring at the ground.
Shaking his head.
Unable to believe.

MANTHA left the blond-haired skuller behind, and reunited with her husband, Hurnarth, who bore an unwieldy-looking wooden beam. Splinters hung off its charred, chewed-up shape, and there were a few nails sticking out. She knew that—if he intended—Hurnarth could do quite some damage with that piece of wood.

But he wouldn't hurt her.

Of course, like all men, he was emotionally distant; never sharing his thoughts and feelings unless they were in the form of ready-made, non-negotiable decisions.

But he had never raised so much as an eyebrow to her.

He *respected* her.

Although Hurnarth spoke to Mantha, she knew that she was only a convenient centre point, and that the true recipients of his words were meant to be the children.

Sometimes, she also believed that Hurnarth saw her as nothing more than an extension of the children; as if some kind of unshakable innocence clung to her.

"The approaching hordes," Hurnarth said, "they come to us bearing the same news—that they've passed through the same tragedy. Endmere has burned down, too.

"Gwindermere?" Mantha pitched in, thinking of the other village close by.

Hurnarth shook his head. "They didn't say anything . . . I would have to ask them . . . we're the only ones." He met Mantha's gaze straight-on this time. "And I don't believe this to be the work of the gods."

Mantha felt a chill pass through her blood. She squeezed Ay'mar closer to her side, more for her own comfort than Ay'mar's, and, indeed, as she did so, Ay'mar wriggled, apparently wishing to be freed. But Mantha clung on. "You mean . . ." Mantha said, but added nothing more.

Hurnarth glanced over the children, almost a reprimand meant for her. But when he turned his attention back it was only to give a firm nod.

The unspoken word was, of course, *witchcraft . . . wizardry . . .* these things, these sorts of fires, didn't start from a poorly minded furnace; no, with or without magic, they were deliberately set so that they might cause the greatest amount of destruction possible.

Another chill ran down Mantha's spine. "What do they propose?"

Before Hurnarth could answer, Mantha saw that others were streaming in around the wall of the stables. Other *skullers*. When they met the eyes of the villagers of Quagsmile, they didn't so much as nod. Their expressions carried a sort of sombre apology.

Two of the skullers helped the blond skuller to his feet.

"Come on, Rut," one of them said, "let's get you some hot soup, hmm?"

With the rest of her family, Mantha watched the skullers take away the blond man.

The ones who escorted the blond man seemed just as dejected as the blond man himself, only that they chose not to display their state of mind so openly.

Once they had slipped away, around the corner, she turned back to Hurnarth. "What is it?" she asked. "What did they *say*?"

Hurnarth didn't meet her eye. He continued to stare on after the skullers as they departed. She wondered if he had spotted some ash floating in the air. Perhaps he was transfixed by it. Or maybe his mind was simply filled with panicked recollections of the night before. Whatever it was, he spoke evenly, calmly, "They wish to travel to Ilsnare to seek refuge." Now he did turn to her, and she saw that there was a certain weariness in his eye. "It's the safest place for us now—now that Quagsmile is gone."

Mantha wished to cry out at him, to tell him that he was speaking *nonsense* . . . that they were still *standing* in Quagsmile . . . but, at the same time, she knew she had to acknowledge the truth.

Even if they did rebuild here, there would be no guarantee that it would last; that the danger—*unvanquished by the Royal Guards of Ilsnare*—would remain out there; in the darkness, ready to befall them at a moment of its choosing.

No, she knew that what Hurnarth said was true.

And that, already, the decision had been made.

"I shall walk at your side, my husband."

Hurnarth betrayed no emotion, only giving a vague grunt from the back of his throat by way of reply. He turned away from her, apparently leading them all—*his family*—off towards the others.

As Mantha shepherded her children after their father—her *husband*—she snuck a final glance back over her shoulder. There she saw Fliggabard, crouched down, peeling back the blanket which concealed one of the horse's corpses.

He was almost like a child now; with that same, boyish curiosity.

When she turned her attention back front and centre—to the long road ahead—she couldn't help but think that she had left all of those fantasies behind now.

Where they belonged for a mother, dedicated to her duty:

In the past.

THE WHOMPING WHISTLE

I

OUTSIDE, the wind swept the red dust off the road and up into tiny tornadoes. And the tornadoes swept their way over the dusty road. Dragging it up, throwing it down. Rattling as it rolled back along the ground.

The smell of rain was thick in the air, just as it always was around the foothills of the Sable Mountains.

Earlier in the day, back in the morning, when the day had been new, the air had had a fresh snap to it. From the dew-stained long grasses. But the humidity had stripped away that moisture now.

Sucked all the grasses clean.

And left the air arid and empty.

And yet, crushingly thick and unwieldy.

That humidity had a habit of sucking up all Gi'usca's energy, of draining her. It was only when the moon reappeared on the horizon that she began to feel better.

When she began to feel like she was being *recharged*.

Recently she'd noticed, on her way back from school, in the fading sunlight, how she'd sensed a *prickling* sensation through her veins.

Not totally unpleasant.

But *odd*.

She had wondered whether she should seek out a wise woman.

Go and ask her about what she was feeling.

But she was afraid.

And, in any case, she wouldn't allow herself to fall ill.

Not when her little sis was at home.

Not when *she* was the one to take care of her.

A little way off, deeper into the foothills of the Sable Mountains, the wolves had begun to howl. Their voices shredded through the twilight sky, as the sun dipped down below the horizon. Gone till tomorrow. And when it returned it would bring with it a little more life, a little more vitality, to the plains.

And that could only be a good thing.

Tonight was a night to throw the windows wide, and not to draw the curtains.

A night to let in whatever light breeze might come off the Sable Mountains, to invite it in with wide-open arms.

But, most likely, that was just optimistic thinking.

Because, as Gi'usca well knew, the night would just be as thick, and as heavy, and as intolerable as it always was.

Because tonight was Midsummer's Day. The night when the working hands hit her family's little tavern, *The Whomping Whistle.* The night when the men, with their harden biceps, and flat stomachs, came all rampaging into the place, drinking up every last drop of brandy wine and ale they could snaggle their lips around.

Their tongues too, if they got the chance.

And her pa, why, he'd let them all inside.

Not much she could do about that.

Except stay up here, safe in the bedroom she shared with her little sis, Hyra, and wait out the night's 'festivities.'

Just like every day, Gi'usca had been over to the nearby village, been to school with her teacher there. She was now the oldest in her class by at least two summers. Though she caught an awful lot of glances from her classmates, she couldn't care less.

She wanted to get herself an education.

Get *out* of The Whomping Whistle.

This place just in the middle of nowhere.

Away from her nowhere pa too.

Maybe, if she just worked out what to do, she could take her little sis with her too.

But now she was just dreaming.

And if there was one thing that she had little time to do, it was dream.

As she packed up the few books she'd scrabbled together, that she'd bought with the few grung her pa had thought to toss her, she threw her plaits over her shoulder and wiped the perspiration off her forehead with the sleeve of her dress.

That was another thing she copped it for. Wearing a dress to school. This past year she'd noticed the wolf whistles from the working hands, and the winks from the braver ones.

But she just brushed it off, just like she brushed everything else off.

She had her mind set on getting an education, and she just couldn't care less what she had to put up with to get it.

Her little sis, Hyra, was lying on her back, on her bed, and staring up at the ceiling. Barely seven summers old. She was humming to herself lightly under her breath. Kicking her feet against the footboard of her bed. And, Gi'usca was certain, she had no idea at all what kind of night their pa's little tavern was set for.

This night rolled around every year. Like clockwork.

Tick-tick, tick-tick.

The day the working hands termed 'bringing in the yield.'

The last real day of work in the year.

And the day that all the working hands received their winter's supplement. The grung that would keep them and their families going through the long hard winter.

Keep them from starvation, and who knew what else.

Last time out they'd smashed up half of *The Whomping Whistle*.

That was no exaggeration either.

Gi'usca remembered that when she'd gone down in the morning she'd found every single bar stool in the place reduced to kindling.

Ale pooled all over the floor. Reeking to the high heavens.

She still caught a trace of that sour tang at the back of her mouth just thinking about it.

Felt a woozy chill pass through her chest.

And the piping. Somehow, she didn't know how . . . well, she guessed she had some sort of idea . . . but the working hands had managed to steal their way behind the bar, and they'd apparently made a game of kicking the water pipes into oblivion.

And water had spilled out all over.

It had been then when she'd discovered her pa down there. Lying on his back. Snoring away. Hands clasped on his ale-stained shirt. A slight smile tracing his lips.

She had wanted to kick *him* then.

But she had held herself back.

Soothed herself by assuring herself that, someday, she would escape all of this. Find somewhere new.

There was no other choice.

That day she had simply bucked on out of *The Whomping Whistle*, gone off to school. But, ever since that day, she'd kept an extra-specially close eye on her pa, and what he got up to.

Because she had to look out for Hyra's safety, as well as her own.

That was the most important thing.

Tonight, though, that was what she'd have to contend with.

But the question was *how?*

Could she steal herself and Hyra out of the house? Go across the plains, head off to the village—the village where Gi'usca went to school?

No, it was too late now.

The dusk was reeling in.

And this being just about the most dangerous day of the year for a pair of unchaperoned young ladies to be out on the roads, what with half-drunk—or *full*-drunk—working hands barrelling from tavern to tavern.

Drinking each one dry as they went.

The only other option might be for her to grab one of those tents her pa kept down in the basement. Maybe she could steal them out to the foothills of the Sable Mountains.

At least there they might be safe from any wandering, drunken working hands.

But what other creatures of the night would they have to contend with out there?

The more that Gi'usca thought about it, the more she drove her brains, the more it appeared to her that there *was* no other option.

That they'd have to batten down the hatches and stay put.

Sit the night out just like a storm.

Once again, she looked to Hyra, lying there, babbling away in that babyish voice of hers. Maybe stuck in some imaginary world.

Gi'usca wished she could join her. But she was too old for that baby stuff now. She couldn't simply shut her eyes and *pretend* she was somewhere else.

Because she knew that she was *here*.

And now this room was her prison.

As she stood at the window, gazing hard at the dust still being swept up in the wind, twirling upwards in the fading light in the sky, she wished for a storm.

Maybe if she just thought about it hard enough one would come.

But now she was just hoping.

Praying.

And her pa calling up the stairs put a stop to even that.

2

"'USCA! 'Usca!"

Gods, how she hated that name her pa had for her. He had been the one that'd given her all three syllables, so why did he see the need to cut one of them off?

Did he think the 'Gi' was unnecessary now?

She felt her heart tick in her throat and waited. She made a point of never responding to people *shouting* or *bellowing* at her. If it was truly important then he could come up here and speak to her in a normal way.

Like a normal father.

She heard the creaking of the stairs. A mumbled swearword or two. And the snorting back of phlegm.

Sometimes she had to admit to herself that her pa disgusted her. But she would never say so much out loud. No matter what trouble her pa got her and her sister into, no matter how much he drank, and made squeezing every last grung his life's work, Gi'usca knew she'd still have that same unshakable biological urge to *love* him.

Whatever *that* meant.

More creaking of stairs. And then the turn of the doorknob. And he stood in the doorway, wiggling his nose as if trying to separate a particular odour from the room.

Maybe he was suspicious.

Maybe he'd got it into his thick head—*finally!*—that Gi'usca might do what she'd been planning for so long now. Do the *right* thing, and get herself and her sister as far away from *The Whomping Whistle* as she could manage.

His cheeks were flushed and he swayed from side to side a

little. His ogling eyes wobbled about their sockets and his Adam's apple seemed to bulge.

That wretched stench of ale wafted into the room, along with the body odour, the slick, too-salty sweat.

Yes, he'd certainly been at the drink *tonight*.

"'Usca," he said, steadying himself against the doorjamb, "wan' you . . . wan' you—"

His cheeks bulged and Gi'usca feared for the worst.

But it was just gas and he brought his clenched fist up to his pert lips, as if it might prevent the burp escaping.

Or maybe he was accidently showing a shred of grace. That *slight* grace that he reserved for people outside the household. For the patrons of *The Whomping Whistle* . . .

He caught a hold of himself and continued, "Wan' you to help me out to . . . tonight."

It was like someone had cast a hex over her. Sent ice flooding through her blood. And direct up to her heart. Her first reaction was that she had misheard him.

But he stood there, in the doorway, eyes set on her. And she knew that she had heard him just fine.

"I . . . I . . ." she started.

He sucked up air, wiped the perspiration from his face with the sleeve of his tunic, and then said, "Viddy's not comin'. Can't make it. Need *you*."

As he said 'you' his hold on the doorjamb slipped and he stumbled forwards a step. But he caught himself before he tumbled to the ground.

Viddy was the kid from the nearby village her pa hired. Brought in to help him on the busier nights.

But Gi'usca knew that 'help' was a pretty generous way of putting it since, from her experience, whenever she'd snuck downstairs in the early hours, she'd seen Viddy tending bar, dark circles about his eyes, and her pa sleeping on his crossed arms at one of the tables in the corner of the tavern.

Her pa shifted his gaze over to Hyra. His cheeks split with a smile. He took several wobbly steps over towards her. To where she still lay on the bed, still quietly mumbling to herself, off in her own world. "My lar-vuh-*ly*," he said, opening his arms wide.

Hyra stayed stock still as he hugged her.

Gi'usca felt herself tense up. She fixed her gaze on him. Dared him to startle her.

Hyra might be *his* daughter, but Gi'usca was determined that she would be the one to protect her. The only one in *this* house capable of protecting her.

A few seconds later and her pa broke off the cuddle.

Gi'usca allowed herself to relax. No use using up all her emotional energy so quickly. She had a long night ahead of her. A long night when she'd need to keep her wits sharp, and her muscles supple.

Ready to knock sense into any working hand that she caught going astray. Any working hand that took a wrong turn and decided on heading up the stairs.

Her pa rose back up. Fixed her with a stare. He twitched his nose again. Snorted back a little more phlegm.

Out on the horizon, she could hear the howling of the wolves. But she forced herself to focus on her pa. Because this was what needed her attention right now.

"I won't do it," Gi'usca said.

Her pa continued to stare at her. Apparently unmoved. Just neutral. No smile. No frown. No nothing.

And Gi'usca knew that she had to be careful. When her pa was this kind of drunk she had to be careful. And she had to keep Hyra close by.

"Whatcha say?"

"Not doing it."

Another snort. And then a hard glare. "Who'ya think puts food on tha table? Who'ya think keeps tha chill outta your bedroom, eh? Who'ya think?"

Gi'usca looked over at Hyra. Readying herself. If he got violent. If he *tried* anything, then she would rush over to Hyra, protect her. And, if it came to it, she would tell Hyra to run.

Tell her to get out of the tavern.

And to run away along the road.

To go get help.

Or just for her to *escape*.

Gi'usca shook her head.

Her pa held that frown another second or so. Then he shifted to a faint grin. Those rosy cheeks of his flared up. His eyes caught a little twinkle to them. And Gi'usca was sure she saw a little youth there. Saw a little of what might've seemed attractive about him to her ma.

Gods rest her soul.

"Come on, larv-*ly*, it'll be okay."

Again, Gi'usca shook her head.

His grin widened. "I promise ya. Ya think I'd bring my eldest daughta into some kinda danger, or what?"

Gi'usca had an answer to that on the tip of her tongue. But she didn't allow it to pass by her lips. She knew it would just make things worse.

Might bundle him up into a rage.

And she couldn't allow that.

When he got in a rage, he got unpredictable.

And she liked him predictable.

"I . . . I don't know," Gi'usca said, already feeling her indecision coming out in her tone.

When his grin grew wider still she knew that he'd picked up

on it, and that he was on the brink of winning the argument. "Tell ya what," her pa said, "you thinka any trouble, or something, or whatever, and you jus' come to me, eh? It'll be fine. Promise ya that."

Gi'usca looked back over to Hyra. Saw that she was back to mumbling to herself. Staring at the ceiling.

The most important thing to do now was to placate her pa. She couldn't have him getting angry. It'd be bad enough with those raving working hands later.

She met her pa's eye and knew her answer. But she could hardly speak it. ". . . All right," she said, and immediately began to regret it.

3

G I'USCA had worked the bar all her life it seemed. But only ever in the daytime. When she'd been off school for whatever reason. Or in the worst of winter when the school shut up.

It was different at night-time, though.

There was no way of telling just who might show up in the night-time.

Though, tonight, of all nights, at least she had an inkling of what to expect.

Soon after she'd come down from the bedroom she shared with her sis, she'd taken up behind the bar, seen to washing up the last of the flagons. Getting them all set for when the working hands came tumbling through the door.

She felt the cold gush of water from the stone taps against her skin. It soothed her a little. Seemed to help to settle her throbbing heart, and her gushing blood.

When she took a drink of the water it tasted metallic and bitter.

But she thought it was more likely just her.

Her anxious anticipation for the night ahead.

The very worst of it, though, was the stench of ale which clung the bar room. She knew that she would never fully get that smell out of her mind.

It would follow her till the end of her days.

And whenever she smelled it later, it would make her gut wrench.

After tonight, she resolved to take steps towards getting herself, and her sis, away from *The Whomping Whistle*. She would wait till her pa had passed out. Wait till it was early in the morning, and she could be certain the working hands had all passed out too.

Then they'd go together.

Over to the village where she went to school.

And she'd take things from there.

As she listened the howl of the wolves up in the Sable Mountains drifting in through the open door of the tavern, she noticed that there was a patron in the corner.

A man she hadn't noticed before.

He already had a flagon set before him.

And he wore a brown cloak, the hood draped over his head, his face cast in shadow.

A hobblesman.

One of those aimless drifters. The men that bobbed from one place to the next. No direction. They were marked out with those cloaks. Those brown cloaks. The ones that the monks up in the Sable Mountains—in the monastery known as Ravensbark—would hand out to passing 'lost' men.

Or to ones who had become corrupted by magic.

Or that was what her teacher in the village had instructed her.

But she had never seen one before. Let alone met with one personally.

Her pa had already served him, though. So she had no need to speak to him. And, in a way, she was quite glad.

Something about the way she couldn't see the man's face unsettled her. Caused her gut to stir a little. Brought on that prickling sensation in her veins.

That sensation she'd learned to trust as a warning for bad things about to come.

And so she made herself busy at the bar, till she heard those bawdy songs ripple through the air. First as a whisper. An afterthought drifting in on the breeze. And then an outright cry through the air. One which she could feel shaking the floorboards of the tavern.

And shaking her bones.

She looked over the bar. To the stacked flagons. To all the preparation she'd put into this.

And then she looked about her.

Her father wasn't anywhere to be seen.

What a surprise.

She guessed she'd just have to contend with all these working hands alone.

4

G I'USCA heard the cartwheels clatter along on the road outside. And the song reaching fever-pitch. She couldn't separate the individual words of the song. It was all so slurred.

Incomprehensible.

And then, with one—apparently—*final* cheer, she heard the *thunk* of several boots all landing out on the hard ground outside *The Whomping Whistle*.

This was it.

No getting away now.

She did her best to smile. To stir some semblance of confidence. Because, truth told, she was frightened totally stiff by the whole prospect.

Terrified of what might be about to happen.

She reminded herself of Hyra.

She had to think of Hyra.

She was the only one that mattered.

The only one she had to keep safe.

The first working hand shifted in through the door. He wore ragged, green-brown trousers, stained with grass, and who knew what else. He had sandy hair and delicate features. A thin nose. And freckles dotting each cheek.

Gi'usca felt herself calm a little.

And then he smiled.

He had more abscess teeth than she could count. Or maybe he spoke so swiftly that she never got a chance. "What 'av we 'ere then, eh? *Girly*, eh? *Girly, girly?*" he said, grinning like an idiot.

She wanted to answer him. To tell him that, yes, he was correct, that she *was* a 'girly,' and what of it? But she just kept up that tentative smile of hers, and watched the others as they piled in behind him.

All of them singing their song.

Bellowing at the tops of their voices.

She watched the first working hand soon lose interest in her.

He shifted back round. Went off to join his companions. And all of them threw their arms about one another's shoulders. They formed a ring. And stamped their feet.

The vibrations shuddered through the floor. And up through Gi'usca. She gripped the sturdy edge of the bar tight and gritted her teeth.

Ready to run.

She never thought it would stop.

But it did.

Dozens of scrapes of stool legs later and all the working hands had found themselves a seat, all about a table. And Gi'usca remembered herself.

She went about pulling on the ale barrels. Pouring the thick, honey-coloured stuff into the flagons. Measuring out the number of flagons as compared to the number of working hands.

She scrabbled about in the cupboards and produced a wicker tray which she set all the flagons on top of.

There were fourteen.

Fourteen ales.

For fourteen working hands.

She tried to keep her calm as she made her way over to them. To keep herself inconspicuous. They were singing another song. And belting their fists against the table.

Stamping their feet in time with the song.

As she took another step, she felt the toe of her shoe catch on a loose floorboard. And, before she knew it, she was tumbling forwards.

Could feel the wicker tray slipping from her grasp.

But then hands. Lots of hands.

Hard, calloused. Rough, scratchy. And *strong*.

They gripped her hard. Snaffled her arms, and her belly, and her hips.

And she remained there. Hanging in the air, almost. The hands kept her from falling.

When she glanced up, she saw that another of the working hands had seized hold of the wicker tray with the ales, and kept it from tumbling to the ground.

Kept so much as a single drop of ale from splashing to the floor.

All those grinning faces. And her beating heart. The first working hand she'd seen. With the sandy hair. And how, when all the others had let her go, the sandy-haired working hand hadn't.

His spindly fingers gripped her wrist.

And wouldn't let go at all.

Gi'usca could feel her throat tingle. She wanted to scream. Long and hard. But she felt the ice ripping through her blood. And stopping her.

Just stopping her dead.

Frozen in time.

Everything happened so slowly.

And then, just like magic, she heard her pa's voice.

Steady. Solemn. Authoritative.

Everything she knew he *wasn't*.

But that was what he projected.

Only when the sandy-haired working hand released her wrist did she dare look up. Look to him there. He stood in the doorway. Having come down from upstairs. And he held his hands bunched into fists down at his waist. And she could see the thunder lingering just behind his eyes.

Slowly, the numbness ebbed out of Gi'usca's system. And, even more slowly still, she watched the sandy-haired working hand return to the others. Sink back down onto his stool. Hover above it. Eyes fixed on hers. And then he turned his attention back to his companions.

Back to their songs.

Only when he looked away from her, cracked a smile at his pals and joined in, did Gi'usca feel safe.

As she navigated away from the table of working hands, she took extra-special care with the floorboards. Avoided the ones which jutted up. And she made her way back to the bar. To where her pa stood. Already with a flagon of ale clasped in his fist.

And that look of thunder still spread across his face.

"See to the customer," he said, firmly.

"What?"

Her pa nodded to the corner. To the cloaked man.

To the *hobblesman*.

Gi'usca felt her eyes skitter about. To the taps of ale again. Back to the process. She had to think it through properly. Work out just what she was supposed to do.

This had been so natural before.

But now everything seemed all blurry and confused.

She tried to clear it with a shake of the head.

Yes, that felt better.

A little more *normal*.

She kept her eyes to the floorboards as she ventured past the group of working hands once again, and over to the corner.

Perhaps, on another occasion, she would've felt apprehensive about approaching the hobblesman. It was just that their . . . their *kind* had so much mystery and myth associated with it that it was like a cloud hanging above her.

Just like the humidity that weighed her down.

But, apparently, not tonight.

"Sir?" she said, her voice a little throaty, much deeper than she'd anticipated.

But she liked that sound.

It made her feel a little more confident.

The hobblesman tilted his head back to look up at her. His face still remained stilted in shadow. And she saw that the flagon before him was empty.

She wondered how long it had been empty.

"Can I get you something, sir?"

"Anythin' ta eat?"

She shook her head. "Sorry, the dust balls ate the kitchen a long time back . . ." Then she caught herself, realising that she was making a quip, and knowing that wasn't the right way to speak with a stranger. Hopefully her pa hadn't overheard. "No," she said. "No food."

The hobblesman made a slight grumble, and Gi'usca smiled sympathetically.

"Another drink?" she said.

"Nah," the hobblesman said, getting up to his feet. "Got a little rowdy in here, truth be told."

Gi'usca couldn't help but follow the hobblesman's stare and glance back to the group of working hands. They were banging their fists against the table as they went through yet another song.

"Shoulda realised it was Midsummer's Day," he said. "Musta slipped my mind."

Gi'usca had no idea what she'd been worried about before. About meeting a hobblesman for the first time. He seemed completely normal. Much less scary than the group of working hands, in any case.

She smiled back at him. "Guess I wish it'd slip my mind too, sometimes."

The hobblesman seemed to the staring at her for a long time. From within that hood of his. From out of the shadow which cast itself over his face. She thought she could hear more of his grumbling. No doubt he was a little curmudgeonly.

Like all old people got.

But that didn't mean he was a bad person.

Just tired of the young not knowing how to live most likely.

That was what her school teacher was always going on at her about anyway.

And her school teacher was Gi'usca's main reference point when it came to *old* people.

Or *older* people, since she had no way of seeing the hobblesman's face.

She was thinking up something interesting to say to him, or some apology to blurt out, when he grabbed a hold of her wrist. His fingers just as spindly as that sandy-haired working hand's, but twice as strong.

She felt a flicker pass through her veins. Tickle her heart. And sink her stomach.

When she glanced back over her shoulder, she saw that her pa had slipped out again. Gone off upstairs, or maybe downstairs, to go fetch another barrel of ale.

Or maybe one of the working hands wanted to move onto brandy wine.

Again, she wanted to call out. To scream. But, this time, her mind stepped in rather than her fear. That was what stopped her calling out.

Because she knew it would mean one of the working hands coming to her rescue.

Most likely that sandy-haired working hand.

And she had no intention of giving him—or *any* of them—an incentive to approach her except to say, 'Another one, please, miss.'

Another thing that struck her was how she didn't feel any of the tingling she usually felt through her blood. That sensation that suggested danger ahead.

There was nothing other than surprise within her.

She wasn't *frightened* of the hobblesman.

But she did wish that he would see his way to letting go of her.

When he spoke, his voice was low, cracked, and husky. It reminded Gi'usca of the sound of a barrel of ale being rolled across the tavern floor.

"You've felt it, eh?"

"What?"

"Haven't ya?"

"I . . . I don't know what—"

"Tell me it's true!"

"Please, I—"

"You, you listen ta me, okay? I know what I'm talking about. You take my word for it. And I can smell it. I can smell it on you all right. Smell it mighty strong."

"Smell *what?*" Gi'usca said, her tone lowered to a whisper, just as his was.

"Magic."

"Magic?"

"Hmm."

"I . . . I'm sorry, I just don't understand. At all. I mean . . . sorry, I just—"

The hobblesman produced a crooked finger from the sleeve of his cloak. He waggled the finger as if illustrating a point. "When you need it, you know it's there."

"I . . . I, what?"

But he had nothing more to say. And, just like that, she felt his grip slacken off. And then felt him release her.

He turned his back to her and shuffled out of the door. Out of *The Whomping Whistle*.

And into the darkness.

5

G I'USCA continued to serve the working hands as they asked for more and more ale. She merely poured it out and brought it to their table.

Whenever the sandy-haired working hand tried to meet her eye, she looked away. Turned her attention to another of the working hands.

And she did her best to stay behind the bar all the time she could.

Her pa hadn't shown up at all for about the past hour and she was growing worried, though she knew the truth was that most likely he'd gone off somewhere in a drunken swagger and then collapsed.

Fallen asleep somewhere.

She guessed, most of all, she was afraid for herself.

And for Hyra.

Because she'd counted out nine rounds of ale for the working hands now. And they had yet to pay her. Soon she would have to ask them for their grung.

Trust that they'd give it to *her*: a dainty little, backwater daughter of a landlord.

She wished the hobblesman had stuck around. At least with him sitting off in the corner of the tavern she'd felt somewhat accompanied. Whereas now she felt completely and totally alone.

The working hands sung through the next of their songs, their voices getting louder, their fists pounding harder against the table. And Gi'usca knew the time was coming hard and fast.

She just had to be brave about it.

That was the trick.

Be totally confident and, above all, cool.

She just needed a little frost in her veins.

As she poured out the tenth round of ales, that sandy-haired working hand once again caught her eye. Only, this time, she couldn't look away. It was as if he held her gaze with some invisible force.

That there was some unbreakable bond between them.

And it was then that she knew she was in trouble.

But she just kept on going. Pouring out the ales. Bringing them over to the table. Setting them down before the working hands. Then standing back to watch them sup.

And all the time the sandy-haired working hand stared at her, forced his way into her eyes. And she had hardly taken a step back towards the bar before he snatched her waist, grabbed a hold of her dress and tugged her towards him.

6

HIS warmed-up, ale-stinking breath puffed out before her. And it congealed with the stench of sweat, a hard day's work indeed, all topped off with the light scent of urine and manure which clung to him . . . which clung to *all* of the working hands.

Feeling his grip tighten on her dress, Gi'usca spun around, desperately searching for help.

First to the door, to where the hobblesman had disappeared.

And then back towards the bar, to the stairs, as if she might see her pa, stern-faced and sober, ready to bring a stop to these . . . what did the working hands call this? . . . high spirits?

His body warmth oozed over her. And his breath got all the more rancid. She felt his chest press up between her shoulder blades, and his hard pectoral muscles there.

She knew she would never be able to wriggle out of his grasp.

He was simply too strong.

All of a sudden, the working hands struck up another tune. This time more frantic. Faster. Fists beating the table harder still. The words more lewd. Harder to pick between.

The sandy-haired working hand yanked her arm upwards and twirled her around.

And around.

And around again, in time with the music.

She felt her gut clench. She tasted bile at the back of her throat. And she felt a whirling nausea sinking over her. And threatening to dismiss her to unconsciousness.

She clamped her eyes shut. Felt the sandy-haired working hand clench her hands in his. Continue to spin her around. And the laughter of the working hands.

The clapping hands.

The stamping feet.

The *clink* of the flagons, one on the other.

And the prickle within Gi'usca's veins.

The prickle that became a burn.

And then a frothing sensation.

It was like all the blood had run up to her head. And that it was fizzling her brains. Stewing her mind with its warmth. And it was then that she felt the need to let go.

And so she let go.

7

WITH HER EYES CLOSED, she felt the brightness sting her eyeballs. Saw the impossibly bright redness on the backs of her eyelids. Felt it sting at the tiny muscles within her eye sockets.

And it got cold.

Really cold.

So cold as almost to *burn* right through her.

Only once she'd got over the chill did it occur to her that there were screams. All about her. On all sides. And getting louder all the time.

Men's screams.

The *shattering* of flagons.

And the *splash* of ale everywhere.

She tasted ale on the air. All around her. Like a fine rain on a spring day.

And her heart rumbled on. Harder still.

Until it occurred to her to open her eyes.

The cacophony simmered down to the gentle sounds she was accustomed to.

The bubble of water through pipes. The gentle breeze blowing in the long grasses outside the tavern. And the mournful howl of the wolves so far away in the foothills of the Sable Mountains.

And, with her heart beating hard in her throat, she opened her eyes.

8

THE MEN lay all about her. Mouths latched open. Browned teeth exposed. Tunics soaked in ale, and the odd splash of brandy wine.

Some of them scrabbled backwards, using the heels of their hands, and the heels of their feet.

While others just lay still. Still as death. And just glowered up at her.

And she stood above them all.

She saw the sandy-haired working hand when she looked down.

Down at her feet.

He lay there curled into a *wretched* ball. His hands held up to cover his *wretched* face. With his *wretched* tunic torn from . . . well, from whatever it was that she had done.

Magic . . . it came as a gentle whisper. But she knew it was true.

What else could it have been?

What had the hobblesman told her?

Yes, that was it. Exactly it.

Magic.

9

SHE WONDERED why they weren't running. She knew that if she had had to misfortune to run into a mage that would have been just what she would've done.

But then she remembered.

These men, they were all *drunk*.

Just plain, straight, *blind* drunk.

And so they knew no better. Most likely they just thought this all some illusion. Something that couldn't possibly be happening.

But Gi'usca was certain it *had* happened.

She knew what she had felt flow out from her.

And she was sure the men realised it too.

They seemed to snap to their senses before too long, and she watched them, one by one, as they latched themselves upwards, off the creaking boards of *The Whomping Whistle*, and they stumbled their way out the door.

Out to their waiting horse and cart there.

And, soon enough, it left her only with the sandy-haired working hand. The one who had grabbed her. Who had tried to *dance* with her, if that was what it might be called.

But he hadn't fled like the others. He just coiled up there, in repose, his rosewood eyes wide and staring up at her, as if she was some cursed wolf about to rip his throat out.

She had no intention of doing that.

In any case, she wouldn't have known where to start. What hex to throw. She didn't *know* any hexes, any curses, any charms . . . before today, before the hobblesman, before *right now*, she hadn't known that there was a drop of magical blood in her veins.

But now she knew.

She knew it was there *now*.

His lips parted, but his whole body trembled, and the words he tried to speak to her just came out all garbled, completely incomprehensible.

And she gave up trying to understand him.

She turned on her heel, now feeling brave enough to turn her back to him, and she headed back behind the bar.

As she busied herself with the ale taps, cleaning them with a scrap of material, she was aware of the *snick* and *snap* of the reins coming down on the horses' backs outside.

Of the cart, complete with the working hands, striking out into the night.

Escaping *The Whomping Whistle*.

And she managed to raise a smile.

As she went about her work, she slipped the sandy-blond working hand a word. "You'd better get out sharpish," she said, "else they'll get a long way along the road."

She busied herself with the cleaning, knowing her pa wouldn't bother to do it if she didn't. No doubt he lay off somewhere in the tavern dreaming away with lands of milk and honey and whatnot, on a different plane totally.

She listened for the sounds of the working hand getting to his feet. Of him heading back out of the tavern—his tail between his legs—but they didn't come.

She continued to clean up for another few moments before tossing off a glare in his direction. She felt her chest tighten, because she knew, if she couldn't frighten him off with what she'd just shown, she simply couldn't rely on summoning . . . whatever it had been that she had summoned, all over again.

The working hand continued to stare at her. And then, all at once, appeared to find his wits again. He blinked several times and then somehow tumbled upwards, managing to land on his feet.

And he stood stock still, staring at her. Like a stubborn, skinny rock in the midst of a tempest.

She paused her cleaning. Wondered what would happen now.

He had none of his companions with him.

Now he was all on his own.

And then he seemed to snap out of whatever daze he had been held in. He dug through his tunic, his hand weaving in and out of the material. His eyelids crunching up tight as he searched for something . . . *something.*

A knife? A dagger to run her through with?

Or something incomprehensible to her?

And how would she ready herself?

Because she had no control over her fledgling powers.

And then, from out of his tunic, out of some concealed inner pocket, he withdrew a velvet purse. Sure, sun-faded and weather-beaten, but a *velvet* purse all the same.

And she heard the unmistakable *clink-clink* of grung nestled within.

She watched his Adam's apple bob as he took a swallow and then stepped towards her. She eyed him all the way up to the bar where he set the purse down with a final *clink* and then met her eyes expectantly.

His eyes still swam. The drink eating away at him from the inside. But she knew that, from within, he was staring out at her.

From his soul . . . or whatever she might choose to call it.

"This should cover . . . should cover," he said, taking his time, "should cover *every*thing."

She glanced down at the velvet purse, at the bulge of grung within, and then, as if speaking apart from herself, without having to process the thoughts through her brain at all, she replied, "That looks like the whole of your winter's supplement in there."

The working hand remained still. Then nodded.

She reached out and slid the purse across the bar. Back towards the working hand. "I can't take this. How can you possibly ask me to take this?"

The working hand's eyes swirled about their sockets. Then finally returned to focus. "My . . . my *boys*, they will understand. They will pay me. Just as I've paid you."

Gi'usca considered this for a long while. Thought it through.

After all she had suffered this evening. With the raucous working hands tearing up the tavern, *The Whomping Whistle*—her own *home*—didn't she and her family at the very least deserve to be paid for their trouble?

But it was another thing to take this young working hand's winter's supplement.

His family might starve without it.

She met his eye again.

He gave her a firm nod, turned around, and with a slightly wonky gait, he loped out of the tavern and into the darkness.

Into the night.

10

G I'USCA left the velvet purse up there, on the bar counter, as she continued to clean up the tavern, so that she might sneak off up to bed.

Already she could see the first signs of the sun tracing the horizon, and tomorrow she would have to be back in school. Be back with her teacher.

And with everything she had learned about herself tonight.

She thought about the working hand, and his 'companions', and whether they would really all pitch in to pay him back.

Or would they just take it as a free night's drinking with a bizarre twist towards the end?

She supposed that she would never know.

And she hadn't really any reason to care.

But she supposed that men that held that kind of company— that *relished* it—would always trust in it, look to it to prop themselves up whenever they needed it.

More of a group organism than a collection of individuals.

Who was she to judge, though?

As she finished wiping up the spilled ale and reordering the stools, she blew out the flickering candlelight, and then looked out over the plains, to the rising sun.

And she thought that in only three more seasons, Midsummer's Day would be upon *The Whomping Whistle* again.

Be upon *them* again.

But next time she would be ready.

Well and truly ready.

She swore that much to herself.

BLOODIED SNOW

I

THE WOODS LOOMED all around him.

Louson Dorf felt the winter bite in the air, the frozen breeze chilling his neck, somehow managing to sneak its way past the collar of his tunic. It seemed to run right through his skin, down to his bones. He breathed in the trees, and savoured that pine smell, felt its tang in his nostrils. Although it was early afternoon, they were nearing the middle of winter, and so the light was already fading.

Lou glanced back to his sis, Syre, and watched her crunch her way through the freshly fallen snow, trudging after him slowly.

She wore a winter's cloak made of sheep's wool supplemented by a thick scarf around her neck. She wore gloves too, and a knitted hat which squeezed her inky black hair down in tufts at the side of her face. Her cheeks were red, and her lips, at least to Lou, seemed almost the shade of blueberries.

Lou attempted a smile. "Just a little further on."

She scowled at him and drew her scarf up to cover her nose and mouth, muffling her words. "That's what you said an hour ago." She glanced back over her shoulder, and seemed to grow a little more anxious than belligerent. "It's gonna be dark soon. If we don't turn back now we might not make the camp before nightfall."

Although Lou maintained his smile, he felt his whole body tremble a little.

He told himself that it was just the breeze, that winter chill they'd almost forgotten about since they'd been so far away, but he knew that the real reason was a tiny fear, just there at the back of his mind, ever-present, it seemed.

He reached down to his thigh and felt for the handle of the

Webbing Blade there. The dagger which all his ice magic centred around. The magic which he was learning more about everyday. That same magic which was the only reason he'd felt any confidence whatsoever about making this trip out here . . . with Syre at least.

Because it was one thing for him to risk his own life, but to risk that of his younger sister, that was another matter.

"Where is it anyway?" Syre said.

Lou glanced up ahead, checking out the fresh snow before him. About an hour ago he'd been so certain that this was the way, but now . . . now he wasn't so sure. Everything had begun to look the same. What he was sure he'd recognised last time he'd been here had simply upped and changed on him.

Turned all *unfamiliar* on him.

He glanced to the rock face, the abrupt end to the forest which he had kept to his right along the whole path. He studied the rocks sticking out there and told himself that it was somewhere about here. That they would find it soon. They would find Murch's grave —his short-lived mentor, back when he'd been a skuller: one of those that had watched over these plains, kept track of the cursed animals that lurked at night.

. . . when there had been people living on these plains at all.

His boots had grown damp as they trudged through the forests, and his hunger had snuck up on him with every footstep, and now it was near enough unbearable. They'd left the food back at the camp, up a tree so that no wandering animals would grab it . . . or at least they'd have a tougher time getting their paws on it. And the chill of the northern wind almost outstripped the power of the all-encompassing pine scent of the surrounding trees.

Every time Lou heard the snap of a branch in the distance, he spun round, grabbed hold of the handle of the Webbing Blade and expected to see a cursed bear or wolf lolloping over to them, its eyes bright red with hunger.

As he trudged onwards, listening to his sis's exhausted sighs after every step, he started to fantasise about the shank of meat they had back at the camp waiting for them. Started to think about the smell of the fat burning off, then that sizzle as it dropped into the flames.

And then, just like that, they were there.

This was the place.

The place where they'd buried Murch.

2

J UST LIKE HE REMEMBERED. The rocks all forming an alcove in the hillside. Like the shape of a horse hoof. He felt his throat tighten, the sting in his cheeks ebb away for a moment, and his stomach dipped down low.

This was the place where they'd laid Murch to rest after he'd been ravaged by a cursed bear. And, as he recalled, they'd buried him shallow. Just below the surface. There had been no time for a proper burial, for a hero's burial. No time for one now, either. And just the wrong season. But he'd had to come back here. He'd felt compelled to. And this was the first time since he'd gone away that he'd felt strong enough to come back alone—to make this lonely pilgrimage.

He was aware of Syre at his shoulder, of her heavy breathing, of the warmth of her breath carrying in the air, coming to rest moist against his cheeks. He crouched down, removed his leather glove and set it down on the surface of the virgin snow. Then, hand bare, he clasped his eyes shut and ran his fingertips over the soft snow.

It chilled every nerve in his body. He felt those thousand micro tremors shudder through him. They got so strong that they made his teeth chatter. But he had to do this. This was the reason they'd come all this way.

As he thrust his hand deeper into the snow, he thought he could feel icicles forming there, getting stuck to his skin. He reached to his side for the Webbing Blade, and touched the handle, receiving its own magical chill through his fingertips. That pushed him on, gave him strength to keep reaching through the snow.

And then, just like that, he was touching the frozen earth.

Still with his eyes closed, he just laid his hand there, feeling the stiffness of the ground, trying to imagine the body of Murch buried just below. He had promised himself that he would return one day and dig his body up, take it somewhere to be properly buried. But this wasn't the time. Not with a magical war on the horizon. Heroes could only be buried in peacetime, and that was a long way off. But he would return here, he was sure of it.

He would be back to give this hero his proper burial.

When Syre, standing at his shoulder, lurking back from him, spoke, there was a new shudder in her voice, as if her vocal cords were half-frozen. Perhaps they were, because goodness knew, Lou's were. "What . . . what're you gonna do now?" she said.

Lou just stayed there, his hand touching the frozen earth. And, as his hand got caught in an incessant shudder, he felt a warmth growing in his chest . . . now deeper down, in the pit of his stomach, and he knew that he felt Murch there, his spirit, whatever it was called.

He knew that he felt it.

Back when they'd lived on the plains, not so far from this forest, in the village of Endmere, Murch had been the head skuller —the man in charge of keeping their village safe from the cursed animals which plagued the plains at night, which attacked any humans that strayed out of their settlements.

Murch had been a man of the night.

Almost no one had ever seen him during the day. He had had no reason to get up, to walk around. He had had his groceries delivered to his small hut by the fortification. And then the village had burned down. And they'd had to flee. And then, as they escaped, as Murch and the rest of the skullers, Lou among them, attempted to protect the group exposed on the plains, Murch had been killed by a cursed bear.

The freezing cold of the snow got too much to bear. Lou

opened his eyes and withdrew his hand from the snow. He glanced round at Syre, where she stood still bundled up in her scarf, clutching her cloak to herself tightly and shivering. "Not much to do," Lou said. "Earth's frozen. There's nowhere to bury him."

Syre met his eye, her own eyes shaking just a little in their sockets. "What'd we come here for, then?"

Lou had no way to explain it. He could only go on his own gut reaction, on how he felt. And that was something almost impossible to put into works. And so there wasn't any point trying. In any case, he had to save his energy for the return journey. Most likely they'd get jumped by something, by some *cursed* animal . . . and he would be ready with the Webbing Blade to turn them away, to keep his little sis safe.

Lou rose up from his haunches, and slowly felt a grin forming on his lips. "Just wanted to pay my respects, I guess," he said, then looked off into the depths of the wood, back to their footsteps in the snow. "Wanted to remind myself what really happened."

For a second Lou was sure that Syre was going to respond with some witticism, to give him some biting retort, but, just as he was sure he saw her lips part to do so, she closed them just as quickly, and then smiled back at him.

"Come on," Lou said. "We can make it back to camp before sundown if we hurry—take a look-see if something's eaten that shank."

Syre widened her eyes. "What'd we do then?"

Lou chuckled a little, just a dry chuckle that pretty much died in his throat as soon as he'd uttered it. "Well, I'll have to go out and shoot ourselves something fresh, won't I?"

"But you're awful with a crossbow."

He grabbed her in a playful wrestle, nudged her in the ribs, and then turned her loose. Even despite the long trek, the hours they'd spent going through these forests, trudging through the snow, she raised a giggle and then jigged her way back along the path.

Back along their footprints.

As Lou watched her go, disappearing away from him into the gloom of the forests, he took one final look back to that grave—to Murch's grave. And he told himself that, once everything was over, once the war was won, or lost, he'd be back here to give the guy a proper burial.

He promised himself that.

And, looking over his handprint in the snow, where he'd braved the icy chill to touch the earth piled on top of Murch's body, he felt another of those shudders pass over him. Then he realised that his leather glove still lay down on the snow.

He picked it up, fit it back to his hand, and then stared for a long time at Murch's grave.

"Come on!" Syre called from along the path, now out of sight. "I'll race ya back to the camp!"

Another chill passed through Lou, but this time he ground his teeth and forced it away, and, with a final glance over his shoulder, he made his way along their tracks, heading after Syre, into the depths of the woods, back to camp.

He would be back one day.

He was sure of it.

AUTHOR'S NOTE

Thank you for taking the time to read one of my books. If you would like to hear about my latest releases you can sign up for my newsletter here: www.raymondsflex.com

Thanks for reading!

Raymond S Flex

Blood & Guts & Hexes
A Crystal Kingdom Short Story Collection

www.ingramcontent.com/pod-product-compliance
Lightning Source LLC
Chambersburg PA
CBHW031318280626
47169CB00019B/2133